I0762254

THE WINNING ZONE

Tilak S. Fernando
&
Thomas Umholtz, Jr.

Life is a Game

With or without your knowledge you are participating in continuous challenges to win in the game of life. Whether the game is in sports, business, even gaming, inventing or creating the elements and forces within you can be activated. Tilak has shown me and many others how to open Focus, Fascination and Trust as a direct connection to the Flow. This is an amazing perspective from a man way ahead of this time.

Joe Sugarman
Acclaimed author of *Triggers* and *Success Forces*
Entrepreneur Creator of BluBlocker Sunglasses

Prologue

Mark looked at his boarding pass to confirm the seat number: row 3, seat E, first class. He stowed his luggage and settled into the window seat. He had made it from Manhattan and through JFK with little delay, and in a few hours, he would be touching down in Las Vegas for a one-week break, far away from New York, Wall Street and everything that went with it.

His seatmate arrived and sat down. They acknowledged each other with a nod and a quick hello. Mark took another look at the man and realized it was his college roommate.

"Eric?"

"Mark?"

"Wow, this is amazing! What is it, Eric, ten—no, twelve years! How are you doing?"

"All right. I made it through med school, and I've been a practicing cardiologist for six years. Maybe if I keep practicing, I'll get good at it!"

Mark laughed. Eric's self-deprecating humor had not changed, though he was obviously very successful.

"Yeah, right. You're a genius, Eric. I'm sure you aced it."

"Well, I guess I am doing all right. I have a practice with two other doctors. We have an office in Manhattan and one in Westchester. That keeps me pretty busy. How about you?"

"Do you know what a hedge fund manager does?"

"Not really."

"It's a form of gambling, basically. If I'm doing it right, I make money whether the market goes up or down. I work like a maniac, but I make a lot of money, and it's pretty exciting."

"And what brings you to Las Vegas?"

"Well, I've been working especially hard, and I just finished a big project, so this is a good time for a break. I've got some other stuff on my mind too, so now's an opportunity to clear my head, relieve some stress—you know, feel more like myself again."

"If it were me," said Eric, "I'd go to a sunny island somewhere. Someplace quiet."

"Not me," said Mark, "I'd go crazy. I like to have some excitement, activity, people, and I like to gamble. So I'm going to a sunny island in the desert. And what brings *you* to Vegas?"

"I'm attending a conference. I'm one of the organizers, and I'm giving a talk about some of the recent advances in cardiology and related fields."

"Are you going to do any playing?"

"I won't have any time for that. I don't mind, though. I'm not interested in gambling. You might think you can win, and you might win sometimes, but the laws of probability are against you, and eventually you're going to lose. It's just math. And in any case, it's not a very productive use of one's time."

"That's so funny," said Mark, "You always used to talk about the productive use of your time. Well, Vegas is not productive. I make more money at my job than I do here, that's for sure. It's about the excitement. You have to be a player to understand, and you, my friend, are not a player."

Eric was not offended by this. He was cautious and practical, and he saw no reason to introduce any unnecessary risk or uncertainty into his life, at least not for something as frivolous as gambling. Mark, on the other hand, was a player. He worked with large sums of money and he was not afraid of risk. In fact, he loved risk.

"Eric," he said, "It's not about beating the odds. I'm not going against probability; I'm going *alongside* probability. I can feel what's coming. And if it doesn't feel right, I don't play."

Eric grimaced.

"I'll stick to medicine. The human body is to a great extent predictable. It's self-activating and self-regulating and has very predictable processes. And I try to make it even more predictable, which suits me just fine."

Mark was not at all surprised that Eric was a successful doctor. He had been by far the more studious of the two roommates. His success was expected. Mark, however, was even more financially successful than Eric, and this fact gave Mark great pleasure.

Around them, the cabin buzzed with excitement. The faces of the passengers were flushed with anticipation. A few were visibly and audibly drunk. The two men reminisced over their time together at college and caught up on the last twelve years. A flight attendant brought some single malt scotch, and they were soon feeling expansive.

The two friends drank and ate and talked, and five hours later they began their descent into Las Vegas. They exited the plane together and made their way to the baggage area.

"Let's get together while we're here," said Mark, "I'll show you what I'm talking about. I'll show you how to play."

"I'd like to, but I'm probably going to be busy the whole time."

"When are you flying back?"

"Next Thursday," said Eric.

"Me too! What flight?"

Eric found his ticket and read, "United flight 119, departing 10:45 am."

"You're kidding!"

Eric was stunned, and he began to wonder if this was some kind of trick. Mark was grinning.

"What are the odds?" Mark said, "Or should I say, what is the probability? There's no such thing as chance, Eric. You, me, the plane, the whole thing was meant to happen!"

Eric rolled his eyes. He enjoyed Mark's enthusiasm but talk like this he immediately dismissed as nonsense. Still, it was a remarkable coincidence.

"Well, look," said Mark, "If I don't see you this week, I'll see you on the plane, and I'll show you my winnings. Have some fun while you're here!"

"I'm sure you'll have enough fun for both of us. It was great seeing you, Mark. I'll see you next Thursday."

Mark got a cab and headed for his hotel.

'What *are* the odds?' he thought to himself.

CHAPTER 1

THE FLOW

"The next moment is like a rising wave that is forming and coming towards you."

A cool mist drifted over from the fountains in front of Mark's hotel as he exited his cab. He checked in, went up to his room to shower and change, and then down to the casino. He was savoring the excitement and anticipation of playing, but he was also tired and hungry. It had been a long day ad it was late. Maybe he would just have a bite to eat and go to bed, and start fresh in the morning.

The hotel was palatial in the style of modern Las Vegas. Its cavernous lobby teemed with people, their voices echoing on marble floors, glass sculptures and massive architectural whimsies. Mark crossed in front of the piano lounge, past a fountain and into the hotel's conservatory, a vast skylighted atrium garden that was landscaped and redecorated to reflect the changing seasons and holidays. At present it was themed for Chinese New Year. Enormous coins rose out of elaborate flower beds beneath giant butterflies suspended from the high skylights. Adjacent to the conservatory was a café restaurant. Even at this late hour the café was full to capacity. The only seats were counter seating that looked out into the gardens. Mark had been here before and he knew that the counter seating encouraged conversation, so he picked his spot carefully. He sat down next to a man wearing an expensive sport coat and comfortable shoes. His face had many fine lines, but his hair was thick and dark, with very little gray. He had an air of ease and good humor. The man smiled at Mark as he sat down.

"How are you doing?" he asked.

"Great!"' Mark replied, "Just got here."

"Oh, have you played yet?"

"Not yet."

The man smiled more broadly.

"That's great," he said and leaned toward Mark.

"When you start, when you go to the table, you should go and just sit – sit for about one minute and don't immediately make a bet. Stay one minute without playing. Not every game will let you do this, but if you can do that, it will be very good."

Mark smiled back at the man.

"Oh really? Why's that?"

"You will learn three things: patience, focus and fascination."

Mark had not expected such a specific answer. He repeated the words to himself. He looked at the man. Mark had taken him for a high roller, maybe a diplomat or a movie producer. He enjoyed being around people like this.

"Patience focus and fascination," Mark said aloud.

"Yes," said the man, "and those three things will replace: greed, restlessness and fear."

Again, the answer was more than Mark had expected. He had not been aware of feeling greed, restlessness or fear. But now that the man had said it, he looked at his present circumstances with a new eye. His desire to go to bed and not gamble tonight had an element of fear in it—fear of doing something stupid because he was tired. But another part of him wanted very badly to go right out and start playing. If he were really that tired, why didn't he just get room service and go to bed? Here he was downstairs, not even aware that he had already decided to gamble tonight. The man spoke, and Mark snapped out of his reverie.

"Do you see the flow?" the man asked. "Do you know how to recognize it and move into it? And most importantly, how to stay there?"

Mark was going to ask him what he meant by the flow, but instead he said, "Sometimes I feel like I'm in the zone and I can't lose, but as soon as I think that, it's gone."

The man nodded.

"We actually, most gamblers, most players, not just in gambling but in everything, we are sensing something. There's a difference between sensing and guessing. The difference is, when you sense something, it doesn't come with any language, any words. It's a feeling you get, a direct seeing. When you are guessing, you are talking to yourself. You are having a dialog with yourself. You are telling yourself the probability that red will come, or whatever it is, okay? Guessing, speculating. When you are sensing, on the other hand, it's a spontaneous, immediate *knowing*, which is immediately followed by action, not thought. The mind likes to interpret and guess, that's the habitual pattern. It's conditioning, it's habit, like any habitual pattern in life—it's an addiction. We have an emotional addiction to guessing things."

Mark had never heard it put this way. He laughed.

"Well," he said, "I guess you could say that my entire livelihood is based on guessing – educated guessing, but yep, guessing."

"Are you guessing, or are you sensing?"

"Ah yes, of course. Absolutely. Sensing. Sometimes I'm looking at a deal or a proposal and I see exactly how it's going to go down, and yes, I act immediately, and I'm right."

"That's the beauty," said the man.

A waitress arrived and Mark realized that he had completely forgotten about eating. As he scanned the menu, he reflected on his trip so far. He had been to Las Vegas several times, and each trip had its own flavor, its own sense of adventure. He knew the general contours of a trip to Vegas: a lot of playing in the casino, which he loved. A lot of fine food and drink, maybe some sex, and random interactions with colorful characters such as the gentleman seated beside him. But each trip unfolded in a unique and unexpected way, and that was now happening here: first, his meeting Eric on the plane, and now this man.

The man was eating a salmon salad and drinking a beer. Beyond the counter where they sat, he looked out into the conservatory gardens, thronged with tourists smiling and taking pictures. The sound of fountains merged with the voices and laughter echoing in the garden. Mark also ordered salmon and a beer, and as he turned his attention back to his neighbor, the man immediately resumed speaking.

"It doesn't matter what the game is that you want to play, whether it's on the field playing soccer, in the casino playing roulette, or on your computer playing the stock market. In any game you play, there are rules, there is a purpose or goal, and there is a state we call winning."

"Uh-huh," said Mark.

"There are hundreds, probably thousands, of books guiding you on strategies, equipment and specific rules for roulette, poker, sports betting, horserace betting, the stock market, or whatever your specific game may be. They will give you the mechanics of how to play and win. But as any player knows, there is more to it than just knowing the rules. There is a feeling, a sense, an excitement that envelops you, that I call being in the flow."

"Normally, we are out of focus, unclear. We are distracted by thoughts of work, family, or the player next to us. Anything and everything. It's like having blurred or fuzzy vision. You may experience it as doubt. Alertness, wakefulness and attentiveness will allow you to unfasten and unbuckle from your doubts and distractions. And that is how you are able to see the flow."

Mark thought of his own experiences of doubt, then he pictured himself at the roulette table in a state of alertness, wakefulness and attentiveness. The man continued.

"Fascination is a key to clarity, but that fascination has to erupt in such a way that it will give your whole body a complete charge. You should feel a spotless fascination for what you are about to play. The flow is like a burst of light coming from awareness. It is not just one place, one time. It is all around you, in all directions, all the time. If you are sensitive, you can see the direction of the flow. You can feel it and you can see it, but not with your brain and logic. You feel it with your whole body, your whole being."

"My whole body?"

"Where do you see the flow, from the mind or the body? You will feel it from your very presence. It's the sense of being totally conscious and keenly alert. It's almost like a mood. This sensitivity will make you not just excited, it will make you appreciate that you are able to feel this."

"Appreciation is very important. It is an identification, it is a tenderness, and it will make you understand the very nature of the flow that is coming, to catch it and connect into it."

"This all happens in a stillness, a soundless space within you. And that still, soundless space has no fear or doubt in it, only light as illumination. It illuminates the next moment that is coming. The play to make, the bet to place, is obvious, natural. The flow is a spontaneous, natural motion. It is we who, by thinking and analyzing, create hesitation and struggle."

At this moment, Mark's food arrived. He was thoroughly enjoying himself. At the same time, his mind was formulating questions about this man—who was he, how did he know all this, and why was he telling Mark? But he did not want to interrupt the man's discourse, so he put those questions aside for later. The man set down his beer glass with an expression of satisfaction and continued.

"Before you can win at any game, you have to recognize and understand three very important things: 1) where you are, 2) what you are seeing, and 3) what you are hearing. It is very important for you to understand those three simple things in order to connect to the flow. The flow is actually the very nature of reality, the very nature of our life. The flow is like a wave that is always moving into the next moment."

"I like that image," said Mark, "a wave that's always moving into the next moment. I can visualize that, like in a science fiction movie. Whoosh!"

"Throughout human history, people have tried to predict that next moment, predict the future. In order to have a survival advantage, people have sought to discover a means of connecting to the future. But most of them created an artificial, false connection, which actually backfired. That backfire, of course, only made them angrier, more upset, reducing even further their chances of actually connecting in a real way to the flow."

This particularly caught Mark's attention.

"You know," he said, "I work on Wall Street, and pretty much everything boils down to trying to see the future. We use everything short of a time machine."

He thought for a moment.

"What were those three very important things?"

The man cleared his throat.

"Before you can even think about connecting to the flow, it is very important to understand where you are, what you see, and what you hear. Where are you right now? It's not a geographical location. Are you at ease? Are you distracted? Are you hyper? Are you being bombarded by thoughts? Is your mind obsessing about something you can't get out of? Or are you actually able to feel a connection to your own innocence?"

"My own innocence?"

"Innocence is the manner in which you approached your life as a child. Innocence is an incredible connection to the moment. It puts you into a space of complete fascination, recognition, and acknowledgment. Are you in fascination right now, at this moment, with whatever game you are playing? Or with whatever it is you are thinking? Or whatever it is you are seeing? Or are you actually in a state where you are trying to get something, either through guessing, or through convincing yourself that you know the next hand, or the next color, or the next move that is coming? If you are thinking that you know the next hand that is coming, then you are already in a state of distraction."

"But isn't trying to see the next hand or the next color—isn't that the whole point?"

"The fun actually of the flow is that it's *not* a prediction of the future. It is fascination for an opening that is about to happen. The fun is for you to *see* that opening as it is happening along with you, together. You can't see it before or afterwards, it is only *as it happens* that you can see it."

"So for example, you are playing a chess game, and you are thinking about all the various different moves that are possible, and suddenly you see a new space. That space connects you into the flow, allowing you to see something fresh. And even if your next move involves sacrificing a knight, it will be the *right* move."

Mark had initially taken this man for a loquacious player, perhaps a touch eccentric. But as he kept talking, Mark found himself increasingly engrossed, and he was doing his best to follow the man's ideas.

"Right now, you are thinking about everything with a sense that you are mastering something, that you are in command of the next moment of the flow. You are not. In order to connect to the flow, you have to be at ease. When you are at ease, then you are cool, there is a lightness you feel."

"You have to be light and cool whenever you are playing any game, because the way you connect to the flow is by moving at the same speed as the next moment. You can do this only by having no intention, by just seeing very clearly. When you can see very clearly, then you will feel a fire, a little spark, like a charge. It's just a little flame, because you don't need a huge flame in order to see into the next moment. Moving at the same speed as the next moment is like moving at the speed of light."

Mark laughed, "Whoa, whoa! Should I be taking notes here?"

The man smiled and wagged a finger in the air.

"Coolness is actually a different speed than heat. You have to be cool. If you are playing a game of tennis and waiting to hit the ball, don't work yourself up into a fever or nervousness. Just be cool. When you are cool, then the ball becomes *a single force with you,* together. And in that way, you can hit the tennis ball 110 mph. Normally, that would be impossible. And you can checkmate a chess player who is far more skillful than you. You connect to the flow of a roulette game and feel what color is coming. The red number may have come up eight times, and your mind wants to guess black – don't try to guess! You have to *feel* it. And that feeling, not your mind chatter, will tell you whether it will be black or red. Your feeling is going to *tell* you — it's not a guess. And you have to trust that feeling. It's about trusting, not guessing. And what is trust? Trust is love. If you are in love, you are not feverish. If you are placing a bet with a feverish feeling, then you are going to have an accident."

"Okay," said Mark, "I know about that feeling of knowing what's coming, but it's devilishly tricky sometimes to know if the feeling is real or if I'm actually just guessing. How do I get better at sensing that?"

"The first thing you have to do whenever you are going to play a game—whether it is at the casino or at your job: you have to empty yourself. One way you can empty yourself is by simply changing your breathing. You will be pleasantly surprised at what happens when you change your breathing. Just take a few *very deep* breaths through your mouth. Breathing through your mouth enables you to breathe more deeply, allowing you to take more oxygen into your system. By taking those very deep breaths, it will give you a little spark of fire. And that little fire is good enough for you to *feel* something, and that feeling will spark your whole energy, creating for you a win-win moment right now."

Mark took several long, deep breaths as the man went on.

"Everything happens within a space, so if you want to win at any game, it becomes very important to understand that space. A winning moment comes whenever your guessing and grasping disappear. When your guessing and grasping disappear, then you are in love. It's like slowly building up to a passionate kiss with your lover. A win-win moment is mouth-to-mouth contact with the space of brilliance and intelligence."

Mark laughed at this, and the man smiled.

"The win-win comes because your anxiousness about winning has disappeared. You are relaxed and at ease. And whenever you are at ease, the flow comes to you. The flow is everywhere. But if you are angry, or heavy, or serious, the flow doesn't come to you. If you are upset, don't place any bets. And don't have a drink either, because alcohol will upset your clarity. Just be cool and at ease with your presence."

"Just be cool," said Mark, "but that's not always easy. Not just when I'm angry—sometimes I get excited, I'm happy, actually, but I get excited and I want to charge ahead. I get a kind of momentum."

"Being cool means being patient. But being patient doesn't mean you are putting the brakes on time, it means you are no longer *restraining* time. Patience actually means freedom, opening. That opening is what allows the coolness to come spontaneously."

"That's actually what the flow means within ourselves: spontaneity. Being spontaneous is not the same as being impulsive. Impulsiveness is what comes out of your feverishness, whether you are feeling your feverishness consciously or not. Impulsiveness is actually guessing. Guessing is connected to your past. When you are connected to the flow, you have no sense about your past or your memory, because you are so attracted by the wave of the next moment that is coming. The next moment is like a rising wave that is forming and coming towards you. That's very powerful to see."

"In order for you to win at whatever game you are playing, you have to be calm, cool, and open, like a hollow bamboo. Usually, however, within your being, you are restless. It is your nature to be restless. Your mind is distracted by all these various ideas, thoughts, intentions, motives, attractions, all these things."

"So you are at the casino and you are feeling restless, agitated, and wiped out because you lost the last few games. Most people who you see betting, they have lost a few times before. Now they are thinking, 'I'm smart, I've got it now. Now I can win.' So life comes along in the form of a game and says, 'Okay, I'm going to ask you to place a bet.' And if they are lost in their heads and thinking, 'I've got it. I'm smart now, I know,' then they are going to lose."

"In any game you are playing, it doesn't actually matter how smart you are. What you really have to be is transparent. Transparency means absolute *porosity*. You have to be absolutely porous, holding nothing. That means experiences go through you but leave no residue—no unfinished business. When you are porous, you have no negative inner chatter going on, no negative outer chatter, nothing. Your body is then in an incredible fire with the game you are playing. The game can be chess, it can be bridge, it can be in a casino, it doesn't matter."

"Any game you play, you are playing for the fun of it. You are playing because playing itself arouses and excites you. That should be the only reason for playing any game. Whenever you are playing a game for fun, there is a fire within you that is actually provoking you. That fire is not coming out of your head. It is a fire that is coming out of the very root of your being: sensuousness. Even if the stock market is going crazy, or the people around you at the casino are yelling and screaming, that sensuousness allows you to approach the next moment with calmness and coolness, as if you are making love to your lover. Then you are connected to the flow. It is exciting. Whenever you can see the flow, it is exciting. It's a fascination for the unknown."

Mark repeated the words, "A fascination for the unknown," and looked at the man quizzically.

"The way we developed and evolved as a human species is through fascination and curiosity, a love and excitement for the unknown. That has been the very nature of our evolution for millions of years. That fascination for the unknown is still with you. Whenever you are playing a game, you should be fascinated by the unknown, not be thinking or saying to yourself, 'I know where this is going.' If you can truly be fascinated by the unknown, then you are not outside the flow guessing, you become part of the flow. If your mind keeps guessing, back and forth, red? black? *don't play*. When you are a part of the flow, you never question red or black, you *feel* the unknown, and that allows you to identify the right one."

"In order to have a good life, you have to be daring. Daring means you have to take a chance, take a chance by your own choice. You are *choosing* to be outrageous. That choice comes actually only out of discipline."

"Discipline how?"

"Discipline means non-interference. You don't interfere with what is happening. You don't interfere with others and you don't interfere with yourself. As a simple discipline or exercise, I suggest that you drink a cup of very hot water in the morning and at night. Sip the hot water slowly, and then just go and sit down and place your right palm over your left palm, touching your thumbs together. Just do that, and nothing else, for 10 or 15 minutes. Your mind will want to go crazy, but you are actually cultivating an energy that will come to you later, rewarding your discipline."

"And that will help me connect to the flow?"

"Right now, what you have, consciously and unconsciously, is not a connection to the flow. What you have is wishful thinking and guessing. You are telling yourself or other people 'I can predict the future. I am able to see the future.' Understand something: if you can truly see and predict the future, your life will be very boring! You say, 'Oh, please, just give me a few minutes of that ability!' No. That's cheating. You can never cheat with infinity and space, but, lucky for you, infinity and space love you, they are your friends. You have to learn how to connect to the flow, and that will allow you to play and win at life."

Mark ordered another round of beers.

"Why are you telling me all this?"

"What I am doing is, I am bringing you into a field of play, almost like you are a sacred warrior. This is like a meditation, learning to focus into an incredible spectrum, because that will change your whole energy. Then you are not just playing to win, you are playing for the fun of playing."

"All the times you lost in life it was not fun—that's *why* you lost. You lost because you were not playing for the fun of it. You were playing because you were greedy. You were playing because you wanted to get something. All the times you lost, you lost because you were in a rush, you were feverish. When you are in a rush, that's when you guess. Rushing and guessing bring about the law of reverse effort. Like how trying to sleep will keep you awake."

"In order to sleep, you have to allow the sleep to come to you. It doesn't work to get mad and blame yourself for your inability to sleep. That will keep you awake all night. If you want to have a good night's sleep, then forget about sleep when you are going to bed. If thoughts are rushing madly through your head, then just focus on something that fascinates you, something that is non-personal, non-obsessive. Like the sunrise over the mountains, or elephants, or whatever, it doesn't matter. Some people count sheep, that takes their mind away and they can fall into sleep. One of the best ways to fall asleep is through recalling something in your life that you remember as true love, or as innocence and sweetness, at any age, any time in your life. And that will allow you to go into a space where sleep will then come to you."

"In the same way, when you go to play any kind of game, you have to forget about everything else, clear your mind. If you are playing baseball and you are up to bat, don't be thinking about how you will be running the bases. You have to be in a space of fascination with the ball that is coming toward you. That fascination with the ball will focus your energy and will bring the right fire for you to swing your bat in the right way at the right time to hit the ball square on. That's how you create a win-win situation."

"Mouth-to mouth contact with brilliance, right?" said Mark.

"Playing in that way is almost like making love. It takes two people to make love, and it takes two people or two forces to make a connection—you and the flow that is coming."

"Winning a game is not a matter of guessing or of claiming, 'I will win because I can predict the flow.' No, you can't predict the flow. You have to become one with the flow. Becoming one with the flow will put you into a space of fascination, having a childlike innocence to see something and get excited. The mind, of course, will always want to come into it and play all the old tricks, 'Oh shit, you blew it! You idiot, you did it again.' No, you can't do that. You have to leave all that behind, all your past. Only then are you free to connect to the flow. That flow is always around and within us."

Mark said, "I have a pretty good idea of what you mean by the flow, but it's a very subtle thing, very hard to maintain. What exactly is it, and how is it that we can sense it?"

"There is a space we have that goes out beyond our physical form. A space which is connected to a motion that is beyond our perception. It is part of the future, so moving into that space means moving into the unknown—because it *is* unknown to us. Our own space is unknown to us, but it is connected to other things. You can be hiking out in the woods and suddenly your hair stands up on the back of your neck because you are *sensing* something. That 'something' is connecting to your space, and you can feel that."

"Normally, what we do in any game, with or without our knowledge, is we guess. Whether it is the stock market, or a chess game, or roulette, what we do is, we guess. We don't call it guessing, we call it speculating, thinking, weighing the odds, whatever—but we are guessing. And what actually happens when you guess is, the element earth, the force of the earth, *doesn't know what to do with you.* You have a relationship with the elements, with earth, fire, water, air and space. Guessing means actually you are not at the center of the circle. You are not at the center of the earth, meaning the center of *your* circle, your own body.

Mark snorted and shook his head.

"I'm sorry, you're losing me. This is coming at me pretty fast."

The man nodded.

"What truly matters when you are playing any game is that your windows are open, so to speak. Your windows have to be open in order for you to experience one thing, called *emotional ventilation.* Emotional ventilation is what allows you to feel a coolness in your heart."

"Whenever you are playing a game, do you experience a coolness in your heart? Or are you experiencing a fire, a body heat? Are you hot, or are you cool? In order to win at any game, you have to be *cool.* Whether you are a jockey mounted on a racehorse at the starting gate, or you are playing chess with a grand master, or you are spinning the roulette wheel in a casino, you have to be cool. That coolness means you are moving into the unknown where you are no longer guessing—*you see.*"

Mark was sitting perfectly still, his eyes wide.

"All right!" the man exclaimed. He dropped a hundred-dollar tip on the table, stood up and held out his hand for Mark to high five.

"Okay, buddy, I'll see you!"

Before Mark could say anything, the man had disappeared into the crowd flowing through the gardens. Mark sat immobile, trying to fix in his mind the words he had just heard. After a while, he paid, got up and walked in slow motion back through the casino to the elevators. The carpet in his hallway seemed extraordinarily beautiful. He entered his room, undressed and went immediately to sleep.

CHAPTER 2

INNER VISIONS

"Nothing in life is a big deal and, therefore, nothing is too good to be true."

Eric was seated on a plush sofa in the grand hallway of his hotel's conference center. The wide, high-ceilinged corridor was lined with tall framed mirrors and ornate urns on marble pedestals, in keeping with the hotel's Renaissance theming. It was after midnight. Eric was surrounded by his laptop, his phone and his papers. He had made a detailed list of all the issues that needed to be resolved before the conference opened Monday morning. He had ranked them in order of urgency and was now attempting to systematically resolve each one. At the same time, he was mulling over his own presentation. He was dissatisfied with the text of his talk and wanted to revise it, but at this time he was inundated with scheduling and logistical problems, and any work on the speech would have to wait.

Eric was an orderly and efficient man, very capable of dealing with a multitude of details, but he was finding it hard to concentrate. He was thinking of his old roommate, Mark. Seeing Mark on the flight had provoked Eric. They had been roommates, not best friends, and their personalities were very different. Eric had always disapproved of Mark's light-hearted attitude, but he was also fascinated by it. 'Here I sit,' he thought to himself, 'run ragged by duties and responsibilities, while Mark is off gambling and getting laid, probably. It doesn't seem fair.' Eric had always found his career very fulfilling. He felt that the work he did as a doctor was the highest, best purpose to which he could devote his life. But at this moment there was no joy in it.

His phone buzzed. He looked at the text message. It was another problem. He sighed and leaned back on the couch. The carpeted corridor was quiet. People walked by, singly or in pairs, laminated badges around their necks. As Eric looked around, he realized he was not alone. A man was sitting at the other end of the couch, not five feet away from him. The man was looking at his own phone and smiling. He laughed and looked over at Eric.

"This weather is crazy!" he said.

Eric managed a smile. "Yes."

"Are you here for the cardiology conference?"

"Yes."

"That's fantastic," said the man, "I have always found the heart to be incredibly fascinating."

Eric appreciated the man's comment, but he was in no mood for conversation. He could only think of the emails, calls and texts he needed to make, and the speech he had to rewrite. He looked at his laptop, then smiled half-heartedly at the man.

"I'm just taking care of some last-minute details."

"Of course," said the man, laughing. "You have a lot to do, and not much time."

Eric intended to politely disengage from the man and return to his work, but the man spoke again.

"We so often find that we have all types of blocks, hurdles and problems which interfere with having fun and playing with life."

"Well, I'm not here to have fun. I just have a lot of things to do."

"Is that so? I think there is something that can help you with that."

Eric was becoming annoyed. He didn't see how this man could possibly help him. The man smiled.

"If you take a good look at where you are and what is happening with your life at any given moment, you can probably identify three major forces which hinder your harmonious connection with life."

Eric's annoyance was temporarily suspended as he waited for the man to finish his thought.

"The three major forces are attacks, distractions and distortions. They happen in your consciousness. Since the primary condition of being is consciousness, whatever happens in your consciousness is vital to you. If something happens in your consciousness that takes you away from the natural flow of life within you, it becomes extremely important to return to a state of balance in order to continue your natural flow with life."

Eric knitted his brow. This was something unexpected.

"What do you mean by attacks?"

"An attack can be described as a sudden impact into your awareness. Perhaps someone calls with bad news, or you plan something, and things don't work out the way you want. You get off balance. On top of that, something else doesn't go the way you expected, and you become even further off balance. Anything that catches you by surprise and takes your awareness, stability and energy can be called an attack."

Eric wondered whether this man's sudden appearance should be classified as an attack or a distraction.

"An attack gives the appearance of occurring from outside you. It gives you the illusion that it is an external attack into your being, where you become the victim rather than the creator. However, if you examine it closely, an attack never occurs without your full participation. No attack can ever happen unless you participate in the event. You are not the poor helpless victim of some great external force which causes things to happen without your control or without any connection to you. Although you may feel that you are a helpless victim to your attacks, nevertheless, with or without your knowledge, you take an active role in every attack into your consciousness."

"There are always unexpected events in our lives," said Eric, "so what constitutes an attack, as opposed to just random events?"

"You are not completely stable when an attack happens. In fact, most of the time, you are not in complete stability at all, even though stability is not very difficult to achieve. The more you try to be stable, the more it will elude you. It is very rare to have a full day in which you are very aware and very relaxed at the same time."

"Why is that?"

"If you examine where you are most of the time, you will find that you are preoccupied with some thought or attachment which you are either trying to release, or trying to maintain. Usually you are in a battle to lose, or to hold, a thought, a feeling, or a memory of something someone said or did to you. You are in a grip, a confinement. You are not free and flexible most of the time, so when a sudden impact comes into your consciousness, you are unable to adapt to the situation. Often, because of your conflicts or your constrictions, your awareness can be changed totally without your conscious knowledge."

"When an attack occurs, your lack of awareness evokes an immediate panic response in your consciousness. Your whole system goes into panic the moment an attack happens. The panic then usually results in judgments, and you end up telling yourself things like, 'Something very bad is going to happen,' 'Something even worse is going to happen,' 'I am finished, ' I am helpless,' 'I am worthless.' Whatever the words you choose to use, you set a chain reaction in motion. It is interesting to observe the overall process of what happens to you when an attack into your consciousness occurs."

By now, Eric had forgotten his impatience and was completely engaged with what the man was saying.

"And what is that process?" he asked.

"First, you were not totally alert. You were merely drifting here and there with a thought or a sensation, and you lost your alertness. Suddenly, something happens, which seems to attack you from the outside, entering into your awareness. Next, panic strikes. With the panic, the energetic form of the whole system changes. Your structure changes. Your mood changes. You become depressed, sad or angry. Everything seems to be rushing in your body. Then comes the emotional reaction. Your feelings and judgments arise, carrying with them a sense that something is bad, and that you are worthless. All your senses seem to confirm this. This is what triggers your feelings of helplessness."

"So, how do you deal with it?"

"Obviously, this is an area in which you must be extremely careful. Once this chain of events is triggered by an attack into the consciousness, you have a tendency to rush and do things you later regret. Most of the things you do in a situation like this, you do because your alertness has been distorted."

"You must cultivate your patience in order to handle an attack. Waiting has to come naturally. If you are able to develop your patience, you will then be able to go into silence if an attack is triggered. It is patience alone which permits the attack to pass away without a chain reaction occurring."

"You just wait it out?"

"Since the very nature of reality is change, everything is subject to change. Even an attack can't last forever. Whatever happens in your consciousness happens as a way of changing one thing to another. Usually, because of your panic mechanism, you will find that you allow yourself to be led by the panic into other areas, which can trigger more attacks. Additional distractions and distortions may then join together, making you feel totally helpless in a situation that has occurred due to your lack of awareness."

"An attack is an important phenomenon to study, because it can happen to anyone at any time. Rather than reacting in a way that triggers a chain reaction, you need to learn to observe it and wait until it passes away. You can gain strength and develop an ability to see clearly the challenges in any life situation."

"You just observe?"

"When you judge something negatively in any way, you do not see the actual significance of what is happening. There is nothing insignificant in life. Every moment, every single thing that happens, has a pattern, a significance, a meaning and a reality of its own. Ordinarily, you are not able to see it, because you lose your reality in the confusion you create."

Eric nodded his head and spoke slowly.

"What you're saying is, uh, certainly applicable to what I'm going through. I've been having a lot of doubts about my ability to do everything that needs to be done, or that I would like to do, and a lot of resentment, frankly, that all this seems to fall on *my* shoulders!"

Eric was surprised to hear himself speaking so openly to a total stranger. He quickly regained his professional composure.

"Attacks, that's very interesting. What were the other things you mentioned?"

"The second important force in consciousness is distraction. Distraction, although most easily understood, may be the most difficult hurdle. For example, you may want to concentrate on some important work and a mosquito may come and disturb you. Although it may look like the mosquito is the reason for your inability to concentrate, most of the time you will find that you have created the situation. Knowingly or unknowingly, you may have created enough room for a distraction to occur. Without your conscious knowledge, you may have slowly drifted into areas of fantasy and memory, or you may be having a conversation with yourself, an internal dialogue. You find that you have completely lost the reality of what you are doing or saying."

"A distraction may even come in a disguised way as absentmindedness or forgetfulness. It may drain your energy, when you allow yourself to drift into memory and fantasy, which make you lose the vital forms that are available for your functioning in the moment. There may actually be moments when you find that you want the strength and the ability to think, and it is not available to you."

"Yes, I know that feeling," said Eric.

"If you stop to look, even now, at this moment, you may be engaged in various activities and not focused on a single channel. Your energy then becomes diverted and your consciousness is not truly steady and calm. You lack focus. For your normal functioning, you should strive to be like a hollow bamboo reed, where the air flows through unimpaired. When this occurs, your energy will flow in a streamlined manner into a singular focus, where you are moving with whatever is happening in the moment. This enables you to have more fun and play with life."

The mention of fun and play brought Eric's mind back to Mark. All work and no creative exploration, he thought, makes Eric a dull boy. The man paused, as if to let Eric's thought run its course, then resumed speaking.

"Distraction can be viewed as a force which comes and takes the vitality out of your existence. Unlike an attack into your consciousness, you can usually see a distraction coming. Like a storm or a tornado, you can see it on the horizon."

"As with an attack, a distraction causes you to feel helpless and nearly paralyzed. You are unable to get out of the way or to remove the distraction coming towards you. It can be very subtle. A distraction can even give you a sense of exhilaration, in order to get your attention into something new. You may be carried away into an exciting, stimulating memory, or a fantasy of wishful thoughts and dreams about the future. These may give you a temporary sense of exhilaration. However, the moment the thought is finished, or the act is over, you are left with a greater sense of weakness and drained vitality, which in turn makes you feel even more helpless. It is similar to the effect after a caffeine high or a sugar rush."

"It is interesting to observe how attention can be drawn into an area of seeming excitement for a moment. It becomes analogous to scratching the skin when it is dry. You cannot help scratching, while at the same time you know you should not be doing it. Very subtly, you feel that you have become the victim, and you prolong the thought or the distraction, whereas in reality, you are the one who created it."

Eric asked, "I know that one can make oneself more vulnerable to these attacks and distractions, but is it really accurate to say that we *create* them?"

"Without your conscious knowledge, you are very cunning in your own mental mechanisms. You are not a victim to your distractions; you create them and follow them through. For example, you may be at a point in life when you are seemingly at ease, and suddenly you find that you are actually bored. People often ask what they can do so that they need only two hours of sleep a night, in order to spend the rest of their time in productive activity. In fact, this would make them go crazy, because they would not know what to do with all the time that is left over. They would be bored beyond belief."

"In fact, even now you may not know what to do with yourself, and you may be bored and restless, and unable to use what is available to you. Unwittingly, you slowly drift away to fantasies and memories out of boredom."

"Viewed in this light, you can see that you are not really distracted by an outside force. Instead, you create a distraction purposely, although unconsciously, and then you go with it. It is like you are on one railroad track and you intentionally jump to another track. This happens with or without your knowledge, and sometimes leaves you wondering where you were before and where you are going now. This is one way in which you try to compensate for something that is not happening right now."

Eric asked, "So, we create distractions because we're dissatisfied with what's happening now?"

"There are many ways in which you create distractions. Sometimes you have an inability to see certain things. This creates fear, and fear extinguishes your spontaneity. In order to be spontaneous, you have to flow naturally and without any restriction on your energy. A distraction breaks your supply of energy without your knowledge. You may really want to take off and all systems seem ready. Then suddenly for one reason or another you put on the brakes and tell yourself that something is wrong. For some reason the plane is not flying. You know that the engine is sound, and you cannot figure out why it is not taking off. Without knowing it, you had the brakes on. When you look closely at the brakes you applied, you might recognize that there is still a fear of flying within you. The result of this fear is that you applied the brakes."

"Because of doubt?"

"It is in this very same way that distractions occur. Just when you think you truly want to change and move, you find a seed planted in a deep corner, saying, 'I am not yet ready to mature and blossom. I am not ready to grow.' It is important to observe closely what you think the distraction may be saying to you by the form or forms in which it manifests itself."

Eric shifted in his seat.

"So, a distraction can be telling you something?"

"It is similar to dreams or other symbolic interpretations by which you attempt to understand some of your inner mechanisms. In a distraction, there are always various symbols showing you ways to return to the correct track. It is through your ability to look at and understand these symbols that you will return to your natural vitality and stability."

"Well," said Eric, "this is certainly fascinating. And quite applicable to my present circumstances, just as you said. And what was the third one?"

"The third force is the one that can most deeply alter your life: distortion. Distortions are very, very subtle energies that can come in very friendly ways. They may even come disguised as positive thoughts or affirmations. It is even more important to recognize distortions than it is to recognize attacks and distractions. Distortions are the subtlest forms of energy and can happen in a variety of ways on any occasion."

"Is distortion misinterpretation?"

"Basically, a distortion is suppressed spontaneity. When your spontaneity is suppressed, your creativity becomes crippled. The amount of energy that has been held back has to get out in one way or another. Most of the time it goes out in various forms of non-productive thinking, which cause disharmony within you. One way of looking at distortions is as trapped fear or energy that is blocking the sense of flow or freedom that is always available to us in life."

"Distortion is a force that clouds the clarity of your consciousness. Although it may take various forms, it comes because of your inability to accept things the way they are. The mind creates a triggering, always seeking change. You find that you want to be somebody else or do something better. This results in illusory effects, making certain promises within you, saying there is a better land somewhere else, or a better thing at some other time."

"Wishful thinking?"

"This cripples the forces of energy available to you right now, by projecting your own thoughts into a future event or object. Because of the subtle nature of distortions, it is even more important that you be alert and observant."

"People who have genuinely enjoyed life have really broken the bounds of the known and ventured into the unexplored territory which lies beyond our awareness of the obvious. I call these individuals *warriors*. These people have two major characteristics. One is their childlike ability to see the world and life as it is, and not as it appears according to what we think we know about it."

"This is the moral of the children's tale "The Emperor's New Clothes." In the story, when the emperor walks naked through the streets, only a child proclaims him to be without clothes. The rest of the subjects force themselves to believe that the emperor is royally dressed because they are told that he is wearing his finest new clothes. A child is always innocent, simple. A child always sees the light and not what appears to be the light. A child sees what is there in actuality and not what he or she is told to see. A child's mind is empty, free of habits, ready to accept, and to be open to all possibilities."

"The second characteristic of a warrior is a stability of confidence which he or she maintains within himself or herself. This confidence is an expression of the inner strength which allows him or her to speak out, secure in the knowledge he or she has gathered from learning and life experience. The warrior acts only with spontaneity. This type of energy in a person not only flowers internally but expresses and manifests itself externally as well."

"Looking at all three forces—the attacks, the distractions, and the distortions —the one thing they share is a resulting sense of unworthiness or a helplessness which creates a barrier to your full enjoyment of life. This immediately triggers a set of thoughts within you which tells you that you cannot attain what you want, or that you cannot be totally happy at any time, or that you cannot reach your destination."

"Most frequently, it hinders the creativity and spontaneity within you and upsets your stability, vitality and clarity. When these vital energies are disturbed, you find that the meaning and excitement of life itself becomes distorted. Understanding and becoming aware of the nature of these forces will give you the strength and ability to revitalize and reestablish the energy within you in order to fully appreciate the life within you—the life with which you can play forever."

Eric set aside his laptop and stood up.

"Sir, I'd like to thank you. I feel a lightness that I haven't felt in quite a while. I've been worrying about a lot of things that really aren't that important."

He held out his hand. The man rose and shook it.

"Nothing in life is a big deal," he said, "and therefore, nothing is too good to be true."

Eric laughed.

"Sir, you are remarkable. Tell me, are you participating in the conference?"

"Yes, I'm doing a seminar right here, now, with you. I call it 'Inner Visions'."

Eric laughed again. To ask the man's name, to press him for the prosaic details of profession, background, education, seemed boorish. Better to let the moment be.

"Thank you," he said once more, "I hope I'll see you again."

"Yes," said the man, "I'm sure you will. Now I think you should go and have a nice, hot bath. Good night."

He clapped Eric on the back and walked away toward the casino.

Eric felt a cool breeze moving through the hallway as he gathered his belongings and headed off to his bath and bed.

CHAPTER 3

CONNECTING TO THE FLOW

"Be ready to receive a pleasant shock and it will come."

Mark awoke the next morning with a momentary sense of confusion, and then remembered that he was in his hotel room, in Las Vegas. Lying in his bed, he recalled the event of the previous night. The flow. Fascination. Spontaneity. Innocence. The man in the café had definitely not been a dream, but this present moment itself felt strangely dreamlike. It was as if he had never awoken in a hotel room before. Ordinarily, he would have eagerly hustled downstairs to the casino, but this morning he savored the anticipation of playing as a pleasure in its own right.

He took his time showering and dressing, and when he arrived downstairs, he scanned the casino floor with a pleasant sense of detachment. People were circulating. Dice, cards and chips were circulating. Everything seemed to in a coordinated motion, even the air around him.

He felt keenly hungry. A long line extended from the entrance to the casino's buffet. He moved past the line and into the VIP lane, where he was greeted and shown in. As he entered, he saw two hotel security men wearing brown blazers and earpieces standing by the cashier's station. They were talking and laughing with the man from the café. He hailed Mark.

"Hey, buddy, how are you doing?"

Mark felt no surprise at seeing him, but great excitement.

"Hey!" he said, "Great to see you again, Mr., ah . . ."

"It's not Mr. 'ah,' it's Mr. 'aha!' said the man and laughed.

"Okay," said Mark, "have it your way. But I really am glad to see you. Would you join me?"

When they had served themselves and settled in a booth, the man again asked Mark how he was doing.

"Fantastic!" said Mark, "You really blew my mind last night. Everything looks different."

"That's great. And did you play?"

"No, that's the thing. Usually when I'm in the casino I'm like a shark—I'm looking for the table where I want to play, where I feel something. But this time it was like I was seeing the whole picture, the whole scene, not just where I was looking to strike."

"That's brilliant. What you were doing was, you were seeing without intention. Usually, when you think about your life, you feel good because you are scheming and planning: today something good is going to happen, or tomorrow something good is going to happen, or in a week something may happen. You are losing the connection to today, to right now, to your presence. You are feeling good as a projection of something you are anticipating. You are not truly appreciating or feeling your presence and enjoying being here right now."

"That's it," said Mark, "that's exactly how it was—I was just enjoying being here right now, without thinking about playing or winning. And I felt very awake and alert."

"To really savor this moment, you have to be very conscious, wide awake. Usually, part of you is still sleeping, not from last night's dreaming or restless sleep. Part of your being is sleepy. Why is that? You are sleepy from your story. Your story is not Sleeping Beauty or Peter Pan, or a James Bond movie where you are being chased. In real life, if you are being chased by enemies, you'll be freaking out. And in real life, you are being chased by swarms of thoughts. There are thoughts and feelings that are chasing you. They are trying to bite you, like mosquitoes."

"In real life you are being swarmed and you are trying to create what? Not happiness, you are trying to create peace, like a balance. You are telling yourself, 'No, no, everything will be okay,' when you know it is not so. You cannot tell yourself anything other than the genuine truth.

Truth is never a statement; truth is how you feel. Truth is always how you feel about your being, your presence."

"You think you are being affected by world affairs and the political situations. You are to a very small extent. They are like the element air around you. The element air is a space in which you are breathing. You are breathing in all kinds of feelings and emotions. At the boundary of the element air is sound. Sound is all the things people are saying and doing. It can be melodies, it can be chaos, whatever you hear. You are choosing to hear what other people are saying and what your mind is telling you. You ask, 'How can I not hear? They are there, they are around me, I have to hear.' No, that's not true. Because if you are really at ease, like a hollow bamboo, then all the sounds just go through you."

"Go through you, meaning they don't have any effect on you?'

"Correct."

"And then you see the flow?"

"This is the most powerful thing to understand about life. Everything that exists, exists only as a flow. Nothing exists as a static, unchanging truth. Everything is going through you. You are a porous being. Everything is going through you. Gravity is not holding you to the ground. Are you kidding? If gravity were holding you to the ground, you would be nailed to the earth, you would not be moving. Gravity is something that is going through you as a cool force. Gravity is not a holding force, it's an attraction. Gravity creates freedom. Gravity means freedom, understand that. It is not how the energy exists, but how it manifests through you that matters."

"So, you mean gravity, like, gives us leverage, lets us do things and not just fly off into space."

"Gravity is not holding you. Gravity is a force. All the forces of life exist with or without you. And your birth, your being here is, of course, a celebration, it's a miracle, though you don't think so. But it is a miracle and it is an incredible, unbelievable thing that it happened that you were born. Your birth itself is a miracle. What if you were not born ever, anywhere? You don't actually think that way. Your birth is a grace. You have to appreciate that you have a body. You have to appreciate how you look. Not like as a rule. There are no sacred rules saying you have to appreciate, you have to recognize, you have to give. Understand that. These are not sacred rules. There *are* sacred rules, however—three of them."

The man looked at Mark.

"By the way, have you called your wife?"

"My wife?"

Mark was sure he had not mentioned his wife, and there was no longer even a tan line where his ring had been.

"I don't think she really wants to hear from me right now."

"You might be surprised. But as I was saying, there are three sacred laws. First one is non-interference—don't interfere. Second is absolute freedom and choice. Third is unconditional love. Got it? At every moment in your life, you have complete freedom to go in any direction you choose. Right now, you have the freedom and choice to freak out about your life. Because why? It has not gone the way you wanted it to go. Who says where you want it to go? Only you say that. You are the one who says, 'I am not there yet.' And you are not in the back seat, asking God or destiny or infinite intelligence, 'Are we there yet?' You are the driver. You are the driver of your vehicle. And in your vehicle, there is no reverse gear. You are saying, 'My car is going in reverse!' No, it's impossible for you to go backward, there is no reverse gear in your vehicle."

"So, I'm always in the driver's seat, however it might seem, because . . ."

"Freedom and choice. Today you can choose to experience your life in pure wonder, or you can choose to be cranky, or you can choose to be depressed. It's up to you. Your mind is telling you, 'Yeah, but there's a lot of things I don't have, so of course I'm depressed.' The truth is, you had a lot of things earlier and you lost them. 'Oh, okay, so I am guilty, I screwed up my life. What am I going to do now?' No. Nobody in your life, including yourself, screwed up your life, because infinite intelligence says that you are part of the whole."

"When one piece of the jigsaw puzzle is about to fall off, the other pieces around it will hold the puzzle piece. It doesn't mean the whole human race is holding you or the forces are holding you. I am telling you that whatever you are feeling as imperfection, impermanence and other things is not stronger than your fascination for life, your love for life. Your appreciation for life, your reverence for life, is always much stronger than the little darkness you see. Always on the Earth, the light is stronger. There are places on the Earth right now where they are sleeping. But even those places that are sleeping, they have a dim light."

"Light never goes totally out, understand that. There is always light. Light can be called in one word: love. Light is actually love. Not romantic or sexual love. Love in a broad sense is waking up. What the light does is, it wakes everything up. It wakes you up. Awakening is pure love. Awakening means you can see things clearly. When you can see things clearly there is a deep joy. Seeing things clearly happens not just through your eyes. It comes through your inner visions, your feelings and everything else. It's very important to see that. And the light is always happening, as a natural flow."

"The Earth is rotating from the west to the east. It doesn't rotate from the south to the north. It doesn't rotate from the east to the west. It is from the west to the east, it's a natural flow. It just happens that way. It's not just the Earth, there is a pattern with all of the solar systems. They are all spinning in the same way. It's not for you to worry about and say, 'Who decided this direction?' There is no direction. The direction only exists because of where we stand right now. In space there are no directions."

"Your life is not actually going from the past to the future. You think that way, you feel that way. Your past is a different lifetime. Your life begins only right now. Right now, fresh. Of course, you cannot deny that you have lived, but that is actually a reverence, to understand and feel it."

"I think I understand what you're saying: your past is what it is, but it doesn't have to affect your life now, because you have complete freedom and choice, even over what you think and feel."

"If you don't feel your life is beginning right now, you won't be riding the surfboard of creation. You are standing on a surfboard called creation. Creation is what is taking you on the waves of wonder. The waves are not time."

"What are the waves?"

"There are three waves. The waves are imperfection, impermanence, and unpredictability. Your life is greeted by imperfection, impermanence, and unpredictability as you go into the future. They are the waves. Waves means uncertainty, that's the fragile nature of your presence, fragile nature of your heart. That fragility is not a weakness. That fragile nature is what allows you to breathe and pulsate with the waves. To realize life is good, to realize life is love, to realize life is adventure, you pulsate. You cannot pulsate without the waves. Without the waves, life will be flat, it will be dull and boring."

"I have enough imperfection and unpredictability; I don't need any more."

"No. That's what you are telling yourself. You always want to reduce the speed of the waves. No. If you reduce the speed of the waves, then you cannot surf. Life is surfing, but not surfing from the horizon into the beach. It's the other way, you are surfing from the beach to the horizon. Surfing from the horizon into the beach means you live your life and you just disappear. From the beach to the horizon means making the impossible possible. And that actually is the exercise that makes you excited that you were born. Your mission is to make the impossible possible, that's the real spice of life. Whatever your mind says—'No, it's impossible,' 'no, you can't do that'—comes because you are self-conscious, and you are misinterpreting the shadow that has fallen over you as your own unworthiness."

"So, we have the waves that are coming at us—imperfection, what are the others?"

"Imperfection, impermanence, and unpredictability."

"And these things make us feel unworthy?"

"Imperfection actually is your friend. Impermanence is your incredible love. Unpredictability is the nature of your heart. Our life is a drive from our birth until we disappear. Just like you have a vehicle not just to go to work, not just to go to Starbucks. Wherever you go, even if you drive from your garage to the car wash and come back, there is a pleasure in driving. There is a pleasure in being carried away. There is a joy in driving. Your heart is always driving. What kind of driving? Searching. You are searching."

"Searching?"

"There are three very powerful things that are happening every day. Number one, searching. Number two, discovery—you are discovering something. And the third one is connecting; you are connecting into a new space. When you connect into a new space, you don't have a memory. Otherwise, you are thinking about your life in the past. If you have search, discovery and connection, you are not in any memory, you are here. You are here, right now. It is like a flower that is waking up. Waking up from what? All the things you are holding."

"What am I holding?"

"You are holding three things without your knowledge. Number one, you are holding heaviness. Number two, you are holding time, through doubting. Number three, you are holding a story—your life story—that says this is too good to be true."

"Ah, okay."

"Now heaviness, very simply put, is undigested energies, undigested food, undigested things. Why do you have undigested food, or heaviness? Because you ate too fast, or you ate food that you are allergic to. You love to do that because you are drawn to sadomasochistic pleasures."

"You don't mean that literally, right?"

"It's like scratching your skin. Or like food that is irritating your bowels. Not exactly your bowels, your guts—your emotional guts. You are attracted to people you are actually allergic to. You are attracted to guys and women who are very good-looking, very appealing, or ideas, or thoughts—very exciting. They could have killed you in the past, but you still keep doing it. Why? Because you got accustomed to having sadomasochistic pleasures."

"Do you mean, things that feel good in the moment, but leave you with bad effects, side effects?"

"Sadomasochistic pleasure is about recycling your own energy. What you need is a brand-new life without dying. And for that you need to be horny for life—not just horny for sex. You can be horny for life only when you don't have any diffused anger. When there is no diffused anger, you experience something else. It's called sweet, silent surrender. Sweet, silent surrender means you have no fights with anything. You don't care. And that makes you very, very powerful."

"You carry wisdom in your body. You carry nonsense in your body. You carry everything in your body. Your body is your pulsating heart. Your guts are your second brain. You have two brains, one in your head, one in your guts. Your guts are your second brain, sending signals that allow you to map out the course of action that you need to follow. Your mind wants to scheme and plan some manipulation so you can have quick money, quick energy, quick this or that. Life is never quick; it does not actually happen in time. Time is with our body. Life is just a blue carpet. There are no red carpets here. It's a blue carpet, emotional carpet."

"What do you mean by blue carpet?" asked Mark.

"We all know what the red carpet is: you are a celebrity, you are rich, beautiful, famous, and everyone is looking at you. We envy these people, even if they may be miserable or feel worthless. The *blue* carpet is where you are not noticed by anyone, nobody is making a big deal about you, but you experience at every moment the deepest appreciation and intimacy with life. And that blue carpet is with you everywhere, always, not just at a film premiere or a big party. Red carpets exist in places like Las Vegas. They are all fake. VIPs, big-shots, comps. There are no comps in life, understand this. There are no comps. You have to earn your freedom. If someone is giving you a comp, 'Oh here, I will treat you to dinner, and you can play some more.' No, never get comps. Earn your freedom, earn your merit, and you will rise. You get comps because they know you are going to give the house the break."

"You don't mean I should literally not take comps from the casino, right? Because . . ."

"I'm speaking about life. 'House' is actually what? It's called karma. Karma is not like you are paying your dues. Karma means every action has an equal and opposite reaction. Karma means cause and effect. Your mission in life is to challenge karma. Challenge cause and effect. And that's what it is you are doing with me, you are challenging the nature of cause and effect, through discovering another sense about who you are."

"Can that really happen?"

"You are not the same man anymore. You had a great past, it's good. That great stuff in the past is not what's going to ignite your life. It's what you are going to do right now. It doesn't matter what you have achieved, it's what you are going to do right now and in the future. Future is not in years, future is the next moment you are breathing. That's the most powerful thing. The future is not actually something you are walking into. It is *coming to you*."

"Wow."

"Your password is: *Something is coming*. 'Something is coming' is a pleasant shock. Be ready to receive a pleasant shock, and it will come. Be ready to receive some weirdos, and your doorbell will ring, and some kind of crazy person will appear at the door. What is coming is your *presence*. It is *you* who is coming, from the future to right now. It's you, not somebody else. Your presence."

Mark had the sensation of being swept away in a current of words and ideas. It was all he could do to absorb each sentence as it came. He felt like he was in uncharted territory. He badly needed to go to the bathroom, but he was afraid of breaking the spell. The man looked at him and his eyes widened.

"This is my invitation to you today. Most of the things you do are very mechanical, very repetitive. Most of the things you do don't open an emotional ventilation, don't make you feel like you are a humble being, don't make you feel that you are very sweet and very fragile. Be fragile enough so that you are like a little breeze that can be carried away by the big breeze. You should be emotionally lighter than a feather, so that you hold no grudges against you or anyone else. You become lighter by releasing anything you are holding against you or anyone else."

"No grudges," said Mark.

"Right now, more than anybody else, you are mad at yourself, because your life did not go the way you wanted it to go. The way it has gone so far is great, you look good and you are happy, but this is not exactly the way you wanted it to be. So, you are pissed with yourself for making a couple of mistakes. That diffused anger is circulating in your gut level and hearing what I am saying and fighting with it. It's saying, 'Okay, that's enough, I have to go to the bathroom.' No, don't go to the bathroom, listen to me for a few more minutes, because you are trying to get out of it."

Mark started to say something, then stayed quiet.

"The truth is, unless you are absolutely kind and loving to yourself, you won't get it. You are not yet absolutely kind to yourself. You are good to other people because they stimulate you, they kiss you, they tell you how wonderful you are, how great you are. They tell you that because they know it will make you feel good, and you will do favors for them. It's not always favors, people may be even genuinely telling you how they feel, but all those things don't really make you humble and excited. They are sweet appreciations, most of them. Some of them are mechanical, and they are nonsense. It doesn't matter whether it is sense or nonsense, they are not what actually releases the diffused anger you have with yourself. It is your own courage that will do this. You need courage to forgive yourself. That forgiving will become a true love."

"I need to forgive myself," Mark examined the words as he spoke them.

"You are mad at yourself at your gut level. You are mad at yourself for the things you did in the last few days, last few months, and many years back. Some of the memories are even gone, because infinite intelligence says you don't have to remember. You did some crazy shit, but you don't have to remember it now. You really hurt yourself, but you have to love yourself in spite of all that."

"Unless you truly love yourself, the light at your gut level will not become a flame. It is not a good or a bad thing. This is the nature of the truth. But the light never dies. The fire can die, but not the light. Fire means energy. Fire means how you feel. Light is actually a force; it doesn't come from you. The force of light is not personal. It is connected to the universe, the pure unconditional love that exists with each and every thing. And that is the one actually — *connecting* – that's why you are with me. Because you were able to let that light fire your energy. The light is actually the very presence of pure reverence to life that exists in every human being and in everything."

"Is that God?"

"That light we can call 'God,' 'Unconditional Love,' 'Intelligence,' 'Nirvana,' whatever name you use to describe it, it's like giving somebody a name. It is not just some thing, it is actually the pure essence of light, that is *you*. The truth is, although you are mad at yourself, you did not mean to hurt yourself or other people. Although you are blaming yourself, you did not mean to hurt yourself. If you were given a chance to relive life you think, 'Oh, I won't do those things again.' No. You will do even worse things! You won't do the same things—you will do other imperfect things."

Mark thought of his wife and the pain he felt each time he remembered certain moments.

"The nature of forgiveness is not actually saying, 'I forgive.' That's just a word we use. That 'forgiveness' is not actually forgiveness. It's like a negotiation. You are telling yourself and others, 'I love you; I forgive you.' That's just a negotiation. Never negotiate with anybody. That's for politicians. When you love, you don't negotiate, you make love. You don't negotiate with your lover, understand. When you are in love with your lover, you never negotiate. You make love. That making love is not just sex. Making love is merging together. You are giving yourself totally into the space."

"Right now, you have dislocations, emotionally, here and there, so you don't feel your power as a great force that exists in the universe. You have to feel your presence as a great force in the whole universe, expanding, evolving at immeasurable speeds. The existence, the force, that's the force of love in a very small particle—smaller than an atom—within you, that exists everywhere in you, not just in one cell."

"I'm sorry, you lost me at the end there."

"You have been challenged and provoked throughout your life, not just now. That is the nature of the ocean: there are always waves. If you see an ocean that has no waves, then you are not on the planet Earth. Wherever you go in the world, the ocean is always moving, at night or daytime. So, this is what I am bringing you into understanding."

"You did not mean to be a humbug, but you became one. You defend your life. You cheat. You lie. You say things you don't mean. But you can come out of that, and let the real forces go through you, in every cell. And you are going to be breathing, not oxygen and nitrogen only. Then you will be breathing pure intelligence. Pure intelligence is not knowledge, it's love, through which you can see everything. You can design unbelievable emotional or physical architecture. You can discover things. You are not just an architect, you are an engineer, you are a doctor, you are an artist, you are everything in one human body. And that's what makes us very, very, supreme. Not supreme as compared to some other law or animals or energy. No. supreme is another word for infinite. Infinite is what we are. What you can be."

"So, this is my invitation for you, to know you can just surrender to your own presence. Surrender to your own innocence. You are like a baby within. You appear like you are a big shot, that's how we do it in our life. But you are an innocent baby. My invitation for you is to make the impossible possible. Your password is '*Making the impossible possible*'."

"I thought my password was 'Something is coming.'"

"You remembered. That's good. In your life, you are not just in a little home. You are in a town or a village, and you are in a country. Your country is connected by the globe, by the ocean, with the world. Our world is spinning with other solar systems, with other planets. And there's a great force happening in this incredible thing wherever you are right now, although you may not feel it that way totally. This is the invitation in our heart, in our life, for you to feel it. And that's when we realize who we are."

Mark sat silently for several seconds before speaking.

"You know, when I met you last night, I thought I might get some good gambling tips. But this—I don't know what to say."

"These are actually the best tips you can get, and you can use them anywhere."

"I see that. But why are you telling me all this? Do you work for the casino?"

The man laughed.

"No, but I'd better let you go. I have to get going, too. Let's have a drink tomorrow. If you are around tomorrow, you can probably find me. Okay, buddy, I'll see you."

He shook Mark's hand, dropped a tip on the table and made his way out.

Mark sat for several minutes, trying to set the man's words in his memory.

"Everything that exists, exists only as a flow."

"At every moment in your life, you have complete freedom to go in any direction you choose."

"Today you can choose to experience your life in pure wonder, or you can choose to be cranky."

"Your life is actually greeted by imperfection, impermanence and unpredictability as you go into the future."

"Your mission is to make the impossible possible."

"Challenge cause and effect."

"Surrender to your innocence. You are like a baby within."

He took a deep breath, stood up and hurried to the men's room.

CHAPTER 4

FOCUS

"One of the most fascinating things about life is you."

Eric awoke the next morning to a ray of sunlight streaming in through a gap in the curtains. He smiled to himself. He had heard last night that it was snowing in New York. He set up the tiny coffee maker in his bathroom and as it percolated, he checked his messages. The news was encouraging. Several of the issues he had been so worried about the night before had already been resolved without his having to take any action. There was still much to do, but he had a full day before the start of the conference, and three days before he was to give his talk. Maybe today he could get some writing done.

But what was it he wanted to say? The text he had prepared was a very competent overview of some of the most notable recent developments in the field of cardiology. There was no reason he couldn't deliver it just as it was. He had given similar talks many times and they had all been well received. But to Eric it seemed a dreary, pointless exercise—a dull recitation of facts. What he felt compelled to deliver was more personal, a statement of purpose. He wanted to connect with the passion and curiosity that had drawn him to medicine in the first place.

He had no appointments until the afternoon. Maybe he could give Mark a call—that would certainly surprise Mark. It was then that he realized he didn't have Mark's number. In their mildly intoxicated state upon arrival, they had forgotten to exchange information. He didn't even know where Mark was staying.

Oh well, he thought, it was better that he use this time to work on his speech, or continue tying up loose ends before the conference opened the next day. But first he had to eat something.

The shops and restaurants were located at the south end of the hotel, which meant that Eric had to pass through the casino. He disliked the noise and confusion of the casino floor, but this morning it was not so bad. Many tables were empty. The dealers smiled at Eric as he passed and gestured to empty chairs. Bossa Nova music played softly in the background.

He heard cheering and looked over at one of the craps tables. A lively crowd surrounded the table and at the edge of the crowd was the man Eric had met the night before. He was standing with his arms folded, watching the game. Eric walked over, feeling rather timid. He was out of his element, and he hesitated to disturb the gentleman, even though he wasn't playing. He came alongside the man, who looked over at him without speaking, then gestured for him to come closer. He leaned in and nodded toward the craps table.

"That woman," he whispered, "Watch."

A woman at the end of the table shook the dice and threw them. The crowd cheered again. Everyone was laughing and smiling.

Eric spoke quietly, "I don't know what's happening."

"That woman has had the dice for about twenty minutes. That's very good."

"Oh," said Eric.

"If you watch, you can see she is having a great time. Also, she has not been here all night. Her energy is fresh."

The woman took the dice again and rolled them down the table.

"Awww," the crowd gave a collective groan.

"What happened?" Eric asked.

"She crapped out. I think you jinxed it, buddy."

"What?" said Eric, with an expression of alarm.

"I'm teasing! Look, see, she lost, but she's still having fun."

The woman smiled as her neighbors around the table congratulated her. The man put a hand on Eric's shoulder, turned and moved away from the table.

"She was having a great time, and winning, because of one thing. Do you know what it is?"

Eric shook his head.

The man said, "She had focus."

"Really?" said Eric, "She was certainly having a good time, but she didn't seem to be concentrating especially hard."

"No," said the man, "When I said 'focus,' you were thinking of 'focus-*ing*.' Do you see the difference?"

"Yes," said Eric excitedly, "*Focusing* is a conscious act, while *focus* is a state of being."

"That's exactly right," said the man, "Focus is not the same as focusing. Focusing is concentrating, making an effort. Focus is something that comes to you naturally, without any effort."

Eric enjoyed hearing words used correctly. He believed that clear speaking meant clear thinking, and he was often dismayed at peoples' careless use of words. It was a special treat for him to hear ideas so well expressed, and he listened eagerly as the man continued speaking.

"Focus happens when you don't have a story behind you. Focus is a connection to the flow, without a story. In that way, you can see focus as fascination. But to see focus as fascination, you need to have something removed from your space. Whenever I ask someone, 'How are you doing?' they say, 'I'm doing good, but there is some stuff I have going on.' There is always some stuff happening. I talked to three people today. The first two said, 'I'm doing good, but I have some stuff happening.' The third guy, when I asked how he was doing, he answered, 'Stunning!' That's great."

"All that stuff that is happening to you in your life is natural, but it stops you from seeing clearly. Focus is actually being centered. It is an opening in which you can experience life very clearly. Otherwise, you are experiencing life through glasses that are smudged. You have to have clean lenses. All the stuff that is happening in your life is nonsense. 'Oh, no, this is very serious,' you will say. No. All the situations that you call serious are natural. Life is beautiful and dazzling in spite of all that you are claiming and blaming. Life is always brilliant and astonishing."

They had been walking seemingly aimlessly, until the man turned a corner and led them down a wide, curved marble staircase to a restaurant on the ground floor of the hotel. They were taken in and seated at a table on the patio. The patio was ringed by a stone balustrade and overlooked a pond surrounded by flower beds. Beyond the pond was the hotel's golf course. The smell of cut grass came to them on the breeze.

"When you are in focus, what you see is not the outside life, what you see is that *you* are magnificent. You are a divine, wonderful person. You have to feel that, you have to see it that way. But you don't see it, because you are not focused. Your attention is going into various other things. This focus I am talking about is not a recognition and an acknowledgement. Normally, what you recognize and acknowledge is that you can make the next few steps freely, because you feel safe and sound, you are okay. That's one of the ways that we move in life. But if you are truly focused, you are never just okay. It doesn't mean you are in danger. Being just okay means you are holding something, you are leaning on something."

"If I understand you," said Eric, "when you say just okay, you mean that we're maintaining ourselves, surviving, but not really breaking free and excelling. Does focus bring that about?"

"One of the most fascinating things about life is *you.* It's not just the life that is around you, it's you. You have to feel that, it's very important. The focus I am talking about is an emotional ignition. It sets you on fire."

"Whatever is happening within you or around you is, in truth, a provocation. It is a provocation, asking you to do something that allows you to really cut through this wall, meaning whatever resistance you have to life. Whatever story you are telling yourself, the flow of life is stronger. The flow of life is stronger than anything. The breeze of the life force is far stronger than anything that you are trying to tell yourself. Stronger than this wall you are creating which looks strong and serious, but which is silly nonsense."

"I understand what you're saying," said Eric, "on a metaphysical level, but on a practical, pragmatic level there are real-life problems that have to be dealt with for one's life to function and not be chaotic."

"The wall is an illusion. You don't feel that you are holding an illusion, you feel they are real situations in life. You feel they are threatening you, telling you that you have either done something wrong, or you have not done what is right. Right and wrong are two different things, so it can tell you that you have done something wrong or you are not doing something right. Both are coming out of one source. You have to see that source in connection with fascination, otherwise what happens is, the element fire, the ignition, doesn't come into play."

"So, it's not the life situations that are the problem, but rather, what we believe about them, is that it?"

"It's very important to understand, you have to be fascinated, not by what you have acquired or achieved, but by what life is presenting to you as a problem, as a situation, as a provocation. If there is no problem, there is no momentum, there is no force in it. You don't want to just live your life and then die."

"All right," said Eric, "I think I understand. I have these real-life problems, and I deal with them, but instead of judging them as bad and undesirable, I take them as an adventure, as a challenge, is that it?"

The man smiled.

"Infinite intelligence says, 'Wake up! I have the energy for you to wake up.' It tells you, 'Notice. Observe. Watch. Witness this.' And then seeing becomes brilliance, and brilliance becomes fascination, and then it is a connection. The most powerful moment in a chess game is when you feel 'Oh my god, I can't move!' When you feel you can't move, all the years of training and fascination and excitement you have for the game—either it can disappear, or it can collect together and come as a ball of fire."

"If focusing is something you *do*, and focus is *not* something you do, then how does it happen?"

"The first part of being in focus is actually the power of seeing. The power to perceive, to notice. It's an emotional watching you should have, not mind chatter. The mind chatter comes because you are trying to compensate, justify, or rationalize whatever you are going through. You are saying, 'Okay, I can settle for less.' Don't do that. Because then you are losing the fire, the momentum."

"So, the first step is simply to see clearly, to be alert and in focus?"

"Yes."

"And then the element fire ignites in your consciousness, and your energy changes, and you feel a great passion, and there's an opening up of your vision. Is that right?"

"You're really staying with me. That's great. And that fire is igniting in all your fascinations for life. You have to perceive and notice and see, and then the energy changes. Whenever you can watch without judgment, the energy changes. The energy then goes into the fire. Fire allows you to see clearly. Then you can comprehend and understand and appreciate. You are conscious, you know what it is. The element fire has taken you over. That is so powerful. When the element fire comes up in any situation, you become charged, then the element water that is around you sends you currents, changes your emotions. It is telling you that now you can discover, make inquiries, find out, 'Oh my god, everything is fine!'"

Eric repeated the words: "Oh my god, everything is fine!" then laughed.

"You are in a charged field. That's the most beautiful part about the true nature of focus. It's an act of emotional intelligence, coming out from the innocence within you. It is passing through all the things that are there. Whenever you are able to see this way, you won't try to rationalize or compensate or justify what has happened. Because then you are just hiding something. There is nothing you have to hide within you. You have hidden from yourself for a long time. You are half what you know as you and half unknown. The unknown part is the most powerful part, because you don't know what it is. There are so many things within you that you don't know."

"My god," said Eric, "that's so true. I always wanted to explore certain things, certain ideas and feelings that are not, maybe, conventional, but I worried that it would take me off my track, make me irrational, make me do something stupid."

"So, most of your life you are just drifting, wandering. You are on an emotional raft, an illusory state. You have to make it into a real speed boat, like a hovercraft, so you can speed upriver, making the impossible possible, and you do that through focus. Focus is the key."

"What keeps me from being in focus?"

"Right now, you are out of focus because you have spent so much time rationalizing and justifying. When you are in the most powerful game of life — which is happening to you right now—you don't have a memory of what has happened to you. You don't have a memory of all your wins and losses. If you are thinking about past wins and losses, you are going to spoil the game taking place right now. The game you're playing right now requires your full attention. That attention is not actually a personal thing. It is something that comes to you every day as connections and ignitions, currents and expansions. Those are all emotions going through you. They are not personal. They are always going through you, but you are lost in daydreaming and fantasies, drifting along on the currents. You have to come out of that in order to see what is actually taking place."

"How do I do that?"

"You need an incredible passion in order to do that. That will bring a very powerful focus. Another word for focus is *opening*. It is a very fascinating, natural thing that comes along. Focus is not something you create artificially. It is very simply and naturally your ability to recognize an opening. You don't create the opening; the opening is always there. The door has been open all your life; you cannot close it. By nature, that door is always open. That's the nature of life. It is more powerful than anything you can imagine. And you are a part of life. You are not a bystander or observer; you are a part of the whole thing. Your essential being is the manifestation of life itself, there is no part of you that is outside of that."

"That's beautiful, but can you be more specific? I need passion, and what else?"

"Focus in your daily life comes through the three 'S's—sensuous, sensory, sensitivity. Sensuous doesn't just mean sexual. It allows you to be sensitive to the space around you. Sensuous energy and feelings are what provide us with the sensitivity to focus and perceive. It is not thinking and thoughts, it is sensuousness."

"Sensuousness is very necessary, because it opens a very powerful connection, not just into your heart, but also your gut level. It actually makes you horny for life. You are fascinated and aroused by life itself. You have to be hungry for life. That hunger is what allows you to enter into a different space. It's an energy, a strength, like a thunder in your heart. That thunder in your heart dismisses all the things that happened in your life, allowing you to see an opening into freshness. That opening is always there, it is unconditional."

"The flow of life is actually a flow of fire. It burns up and eliminates all the refuse that is hanging around your life. This flow contains a fire, but not like a flame, it is an energy that is coming out. The reason the fire is there, the heat and the emotional essence are there, is so that you won't fall asleep. You only need to sleep as a way of restoring your physical body, that's natural. But the fire keeps you from being sleepy emotionally during the day."

Eric was nodding his head rapidly.

"So, focus is not a mental exercise or a discipline—it comes out of an emotional excitement or arousal."

"That's correct. The way you are able to see the focus of life is because it opens windows called *sensing*. What we are doing in the world today is, we are expanding our lives through the senses. We have all these high-tech inventions that have evolved out of our knowledge, but we are also evolving emotionally. We are evolving emotionally and in our senses. Our emotional faculties and our inner visions, our melodies, our touch, and taste, and smell, are also evolving. We are waking up emotionally."

Eric was listening and at the same time he was reliving a moment in his childhood. He had always steered himself away from what he thought of as sentimentality, emotionalism, touchy-feely, fuzzy thinking. But this man was none of those things. He was describing a life where emotion and intellect could enhance each other, and there were no boundaries and limits. Eric felt an upwelling of emotion. He felt dizzy. He felt his heart beating, and he blinked away a tear.

"Remember, focus is not concentration. Focus is sensing. Your sensing is a means of discovering. You are unearthing and bringing to light new ideas, new feelings you never experienced before. This is how you are able to capture the fundamental, elemental nature of intelligence. Intelligence is not something you capture through knowledge or information or memory. Intelligence is not something that has already been known. What has been known is what exists in time. Intelligence is something you capture right now, by breaking through time. It is a sensuous knowing, a sensitivity. True sensuousness is not just about a man or a woman. It is the infinite intelligence that allows you to see *through* time, not just in time. There is nothing actually personal in it."

Eric composed himself to speak.

"I'm sorry, I have to ask you this again—that sounds so beautiful, but how can I live like that?"

"In order to have that, you have to experience a few other very powerful connections. Those connections are coming to you. Focus is something that comes to you when you can leave behind all the things that you are telling yourself, all the stories about your struggling and your past mistakes."

"There's a lot to leave behind."

"Life is always moving forward, like a freeway. There are no rest stops for you to pause and examine your story. Life, the infinite intelligence, keeps on moving, and you have to move with it. It's not that you are in a hurry. There is never any hurry. But the flow never stops. The flow is actually right now coming out of you as very powerful energies called *intentions*. The flow in your heart is the intentions you have. What are your intentions? It doesn't matter what the intentions are. The intelligence and the space never question you."

"Intelligence is not rules or moral judgments. Intelligence actually comes to you as an exposure, a revelation, making known, emotionally, so many things that you have never felt before. Why? Because intelligence is fun. Life is fun. Life is never serious. Life is actually set up for you to let go of all your heaviness, to drop your story and keep moving."

"Life wants me to have fun?"

"Life is always feeding you various currents called transference, transformation, transmission, transcendence. Those are the waves in which you can discover signals, different emotional energies. Your life is actually a voyage, an expedition taking you beyond your horizons. And the waves that are coming toward you are part of an unseen flow. They allow you to modify or convert any challenge, anything that is coming into your life, into a lightness. The element water contains currents that are always taking you to different points of wonder in the ocean. But you have to be daring. You have to be outrageous."

"I've never been daring. I've never been outrageous. It feels like you've opened a window, and I can see very clearly what you're describing, but I can't step into it. I don't know how. I can't let myself go."

"If you do something outrageous, then the innocence within you will come out. Innocence is what allows you to experience the power of trust. Trust is actually illumination, it is not a set of beliefs or understandings. Trust and focus go hand-in-hand. Illumination is what allows you to see that you are fine, and that you can give yourself totally. When you give yourself totally, the waves will take you away."

"I'm sorry to keep asking you the same question, *how*, but how do I give myself totally, how do I connect to the waves?"

"Those waves are always with you, and the Earth is sending you signals to connect. What you connect to is fascination. Your fascination with your own presence makes you pulsate with wonder. Then your appreciation comes into focus, and the lightness you will experience will bring a smile to your face. The element air will then send some of its agents, dispatching various communications for you to articulate and deliver. It will open your eyes to discover and create things you have never seen before. The element air is what opens the emotional space for brilliance to come, through ventilation, making you alive and awake and alert."

Eric felt overwhelmed by a flood of emotion. He struggled to speak.

"I'm not sure what's happening to me. I've been afraid of emotion—I always felt like emotion was the enemy of reason. I feel like I've only been seeing a small portion of reality."

The man took Eric's hand in both of his.

"You don't have to be outrageous and do outrageous things. That will come to you. Just know that it's okay for you to feel everything that is in you. There's no right or wrong. Listen to me now. You are a doctor, right? So, I think tomorrow we should play a round of golf."

Eric laughed.

"I'd love to, but the conference is starting tomorrow and I'm going to be very busy."

"All right, we can play in the evening. Let's meet at the clubhouse at six."

"All right. Six o'clock."

CHAPTER 5

THE SECRET OF IMPERFECTION

"Behind all the challenges and disappointments and frustrations is a wakeup call."

Mark was standing in the lobby, near the entrance to hotel's piano bar. He was staring at a section of wall, down which a thin layer of water cascaded. The wall was black granite, and the water gave it the appearance of a dark, shimmering mirror. Inside the bar, a pianist played standards in a bluesy saunter. Mark gazed at his reflection in the sheet of water. 'Water is emotion,' he thought to himself, 'and I see myself through emotion.' He reached out his hand and put his fingers against the wall. The swiftly moving water ran onto his hand, down his arm and onto his pants and shoes. He jumped back and swore, then laughed.

"You'd better be careful," said a voice behind him.

He turned and saw his anonymous friend, standing with arms folded, regarding him with amusement.

"Oh, you saw that," said Mark, "Wonderful. One of my finer moments. As a matter of fact, I was just thinking about how emotions are like water—they're always flowing, and sometimes they mess up your shoes."

"Very good," said the man, "I think you better have a drink before you hurt yourself."

"A fine idea. Shall we?" He gestured to the piano bar entrance.

They entered and were seated in a circular booth near the front of the bar. They ordered drinks, and the man, who seemed in especially high spirits, asked, "How are you doing?"

Mark shook his head rapidly back and forth.

"I don't know what's going on. This was supposed to be a fun little trip to Vegas, and now I don't know *what* it is. I met this guy from college on the plane—that was remarkable—and then I met you, and you have thoroughly blown my mind—oh, by the way, I called my wife."

"And how was it?"

"It was—I don't know. It wasn't what I expected."

"How so?"

"Well, first of all, she was supposed to come here with me, but we had a fight, and I ended up going by myself. Or did you know that already?"

The man chuckled.

"Yeah, she was pretty mad. We've had fights before, but I'll be honest, I was worried this might be the end. She says I haven't changed at all since we've been married, that I still live exactly like I did before. And she's right. Oh, I can change. The problem is, I immediately change back again!"

"Anyway, I called her, and she didn't seem mad at all. I was expecting to get an earful, but she was talking to me like an old pal."

"That's great," said the man.

"Maybe. It made me nervous. What if she's being nice to me because she doesn't really care anymore—she's already moved on? Or she's planning some kind of revenge!"

The man laughed.

"She feels happy because something is going through you right now, and she is connected to you. She can feel a shift. She's more sensitive than you are."

Mark thought about this and sipped his scotch. Beyond the piano bar the casino patrons circulated in the aisles. A group of women stood in front of the bar entrance, talking to each other and looking at their phones. They all wore very high heels and very short dresses, and as they chatted and swayed Mark's eyes danced along the hemlines of their skirts.

"What you need," said the man, "is some hot sex."

"What?"

"I think for you one woman is not enough. You should get two."

"What?" Mark said again, "are you serious?"

"I am never serious," said the man, "But I'm not kidding. There are no rules that say you can't do this or that. Those are all things you created. Why was marriage created? So, you would have some kind of order and stability in society, for the survival and continuation of the species. In a primitive society, that was necessary, but now you don't need that, and you can truly begin to experience freedom."

"Dude," said Mark, "I can appreciate all that, but seriously, now's not the time. I'm on thin ice here, and I don't need to do anything to screw it up."

"Can you love somebody without holding onto them? If your wife wants to go with another man, can you love her enough to let her, and be happy for her?"

Mark thought for a moment.

"Uh, no."

"That's okay, but it's not love. If your love can be very clean and pure, then you will only want for the other person to be happy, and for them to be free."

"Well, I'm not there yet."

He was still looking at the women.

"Anyway, it's a lot of work to get laid."

"Now you are just rationalizing. But it's okay. Human nature is, we are always seeking, always trying to find."

"To find what?"

"Most of the time you are thinking about sex, money or power, though you may not be thinking about sex, money and power *as such*. You may not be thinking about having sex, you may be thinking about some kind of a connection that will make your life good, a feeling of intimacy and connection. And money means security. You are always scheming and planning about how to get money or something that will bring your life a certain richness or security. Power means you want to experience a sense of your presence as a powerful being in this world. You want people to think you are a great man. Somewhere there is a yearning within you to experience recognition by others."

"Okay," said Mark, "I guess I feel those things."

"These are not good or bad things. There's nothing wrong with it. But they are truly not making you light, they are making you heavy and serious. Whenever you think about getting anything, within yourself there is a seriousness and a heaviness. That heaviness and seriousness *itself* is what blocks you from receiving whatever you want from life and are looking for. What we are looking for can be intimacy, security, or identity, but we are not thinking in those terms. We are trying to have a good time in one way or another."

"I haven't been able to have a good time in a while," said Mark, "though that may be changing. But I feel guilty. How can I have a good time when my life is a mess?"

"The reason you are not truly connecting to the flow of life that can produce security, or connecting to the flow of life that will bring you whatever you want, is that you are being hit by three waves of infinite nature. The infinite nature of life is made out of three things: imperfection, impermanence, and unpredictability."

Mark repeated the words: "Imperfection, impermanence and unpredictability."

"They are not just words. They are forces around you. They are like waves of energy around you that are hitting you. They are taking you from a state of stability into a state of imbalance. Right now, you are in a state of imbalance. That is why you are not at ease. You are not in balance because something about imperfection has touched you in some way or other. Imperfection means, very simply, things are not the way you want them to be."

"A lot of things aren't the way I'd like them to be, so why do certain things put me off balance?"

"When the imperfection touches you, you don't think of it as imperfection at all. You experience imperfection as sadness. Something is making you sad. What is making you sad is, very simply, disappointment. Disappointment is another word for imperfection. Disappointment means it didn't go the way you wanted. Disappointment is actually a surprise, but it's not a pleasant surprise, it's an unpleasant surprise. You are waiting to receive something in life, but when the infinite nature of life hits you with imperfection, you go off-balance, and then you experience imperfection *not* as appreciation, gratitude or wonder, but as sadness. When you are sad, your whole energy contracts. Ordinarily, your energy should just explode and unwind and surf or dance or just fall into somebody's arms. But something happens."

"What happens?"

"Whether you call what is happening a mistake or a disappointment or a frustration, something challenged you. Are you able to wake up to the challenge? If you can wake up to a challenge and ride the wave, then it doesn't matter whatever disappointment or mistake you made. You will not have the same cause and effect of sorrow or going down. Not that you will be happy when receiving bad news or when something bad happens. But when these things happen, we actually contract, and that contraction is a sadness. But the beautiful part is, it is also giving you a wakeup call."

"The sadness, the disappointment, is a wakeup call?"

"Behind all the challenges and disappointments and frustrations is a wakeup call. Emotionally, if you can wake up and see things—not that you will be happy and excited, but it changes the negative energy, negative gravitational force that is trying to pull you down. Instead, you can surf through that, allowing you to come out of it. When imperfection challenges you, it creates doubt in your heart. Doubt is like an emotional virus. When doubt comes, suddenly, all the excitement you had is gone. But all the doubt, all the darkness, is only the absence of light. You can come out of it."

Mark furrowed his brow.

"Okay, let me see if I got this. Imperfection creates disappointment, and sadness, but it doesn't have to. You can take it as a challenge, a wakeup call. That's awesome. What were the other ones you mentioned?"

"The next wave that comes and challenges you is impermanence. Impermanence is different from imperfection. Impermanence tells you; you are not a big deal. You are claiming to the world, I am somebody, I am this or that. Impermanence comes and challenges that. It tells you that you cannot hold anything. Someone that you have been with for years, that you thought would never leave, just leaves, they're gone. That has a huge impact on you. Or you have all these ideas about all the things you are going to do or get, and then the stock market crashes."

"Impermanence means you cannot hold anyone or anything. Nothing stays. You told yourself, 'I am so brilliant, I can see clearly, I can predict, I can see the stock markets, I can see through things.' Like a gambler who says, 'Oh, I know the numbers that will come, I feel that.' No, they are all challenged by impermanence. Impermanence means nothing stays as it is. The moment you feel that you've got it, that you understand, it's gone from your reach."

"And what happens when you get hit by impermanence?"

"Impermanence doesn't make you sad, it makes you furious. You are very angry. You are angry because you thought you could control things. You felt that you could control nature, control your life, control your energy, control your family, control your emotions, control the world, control your thoughts."

"Impermanence comes and tells you; you are nobody. You are a speck of dust in infinity. And that hurts your ego. It has an impact on your security. The impermanence comes and touches you and says, you are not secure. That challenges you, and then you get angry. The anger is diffused. You don't show that you are angry. You may not know that you are angry, but you are truly angry. And like a fog, suddenly the blue sky is gone. It is covered in clouds. The impermanence just comes and says, it is not the way you thought it was. And then you go down."

Mark laughed ruefully.

"Great. Then what?"

"The third thing that comes and really attacks the human heart, the human consciousness, is unpredictability. Unpredictability is very difficult to define. Unpredictability means, suddenly everything changes. Just like the weather can change, anything can change. What actually changes is not only your view, not only what you are holding that went away. Unpredictability comes when you are too sure you are going to win. When you are too sure you are going to have good health, or a great life, or the stock market is in your favor, or you are in love, so certain that this is it—suddenly, along comes unpredictability."

"Imperfection is a distraction, impermanence is a distortion, and unpredictability is an attack. It's like a sudden accident. All the accidents are unpredictable. There are no predictable accidents. Any accident happens because you happened to be in that place. No accident can happen without your participation. Unpredictability means you brought yourself into a place of vulnerability, a fragile energy, and suddenly everything just exploded."

"Unpredictability is an accident, it's not your fault. It's not anybody's fault. But at the same time, you do participate. You create everything in your life. Everything is your creation, including accidents. Unpredictability doesn't create sadness or anger. It leaves you with fear. You are frightened. And you are not going to be spontaneous as a result. Unpredictability challenges you."

"The sorrows you have, the sadness you have, and the anger and fear you have, they are all connected to imperfection, impermanence, and unpredictability. It is because of your lack of awareness about them that you get caught. So, is it possible for you to actually change it? Is it possible you can come into an emotional or mental balance? When imperfection hits you, when impermanence hits you in disguised ways and tries to tease you, when an attack is about to come, can you prevent it? The answer is yes. That is the difference between survival and liberation."

"So, how do I do that?"

"Normally in life, what we do is, we survive. We get by. We get by in two ways. First, by spontaneous adaptation, which means finding a space of safety and freedom. It's like, if somebody throws a rock, you move away from it. The other way we survive the imperfection, impermanence, and unpredictability is through rationalization, justification and compensation. We rationalize, justify, and compensate for whatever happened, emotionally and mentally. We tell a story. We explain why it happened. We create a lot of stories about 'how come' and 'why.' You should never be asking how come and why. If you are trying to answer how come and why, you are recycling your energy. It is only by opening your heart you can go through them. That means living life very lightly, like a cool breeze."

"The truth is, you are not just made out of cells and energy. You are clear light. Meaning, within you there is a space of freedom, almost like a cool breeze. You have an innocent nature, in which your heart is telling you to trust certain feelings that you have, and never fear, and live your life. Going with those feelings is called heart trust. Heart trust is not based on memory or knowledge. It is based on pure recognition and acknowledgment and appreciation for whatever is coming to you right now. If you can recognize, acknowledge and appreciate whatever is coming to you right now, you will turn around any impact, any attack, and that will create a fascination in your heart. You will feel good about it."

"Heart trust," said Mark, "does that mean you don't get upset by whatever's happening? You don't take it personally?"

"Rather than getting angry or sad about something, if you can feel in your heart that this is a wakeup call for you, no matter what happened, then you will rise. You will rise through that moment into vertical ascendance."

"What do you mean by vertical ascendance?"

"All the imperfection, impermanence, and unpredictability happen only on one plane. That can be called the horizontal plane of life. Meaning, connected to the Earth, connected to gravity, connected to survival. If you can somehow or other experience lightness and live your life—not as if there is no past—but live your life as if there is no future. If you can do that, then you are coming out of the horizontal plane into a vertical ascendance. If you can live your life as if there is no future, then, automatically, you are not looking back into your past history. Living right now is the only way to be living without a future. Because then you are living in the absolute appreciation and wonder of this moment."

Mark looked around at the bar patrons, sitting in pools of light conversing, smoking, gesturing. He looked across the table at a stranger talking to him as he daydreamed. The complete novelty of his situation filled him with an intense feeling of immediacy. He had no idea what would happen next.

"At this moment right now in your life, there is something in front of you that is happening which is so exciting and fascinating. It may not appear to be exciting and fascinating, maybe you are just lying down in bed, or just walking. It doesn't have to be counting cash, or making love, or eating something delicious. Those are great moments, but any moment can be a great moment if you are able to participate in the same way as when you are making love or going to sleep or eating something delicious, not worrying about consequences or what will happen in the future."

"Whenever you feel dark or heavy there is always a little space in your heart which is pulsating to capture a little light. The light can come into you. That light is a realization that will go into your whole body. Just a very small realization. The realization is, this moment right now is an incredible moment. It becomes incredible because you happen to be an incredible being connecting into the flow of life. Therefore, this incredible moment, whatever it may be, is just like making love or connecting to anything—it will become an infinite experience. An infinite experience takes away all the little things you worry about, all the things you are fearful or angry about."

"I can feel that, absolutely, right now," said Mark.

"All the things that worry you are very little compared to the great lightness, the great coolness, and the great energy that is around you and in you, pulsating together. It doesn't matter what it is you are worried about or fearful of, the light in your heart, your power of awakening, your power of ascendance, is so much greater."

"Just like the sunrise coming and taking the dark night away, it's the power of light, the power of love, the power of fascination. The excitement that it happened to be you who is you comes and touches you. Let it penetrate you, through recognition, through acknowledgment, into your whole body, and it will run through all the trillions of cells you have, and it will illuminate you and you will light up better than any Christmas tree. You will feel such grace in your heart that you don't care. You don't care about anything anymore. You are not living for a future. You are living for the present, for the joy of your heart. It happened to be you who is you, that's the best news and the greatest sweetness. Then you are saying 'Yes!' to life."

"Yes!" Mark exclaimed, "Yes! Yes! YES!"

CHAPTER 6

THUNDER IN THE HEART

"All the things that are happening with the Earth are also happening within us."

"When I was a kid, there was a park near my elementary school, where I used to spend a lot of time. One day I was there with my dog. I was running, and as I was running, I was feeling my heart beating, boom-boom, boom-boom, boom-boom. It was almost like my heart was a separate entity within me, a living thing within me. I was running, it was beating. Then I remember I was hugging my dog, burying my face in his fur, and I could feel his heart beating too. I looked around at the people in the park and on the street, and—I don't know how to describe it, but it was like I could feel their hearts as well, I could sense them pulsing, beating, every person, every animal, every insect, and I felt connected to them. It was like we were all part of a network, a web, with invisible lines connecting me to every one of them. And it didn't stop there. I had a sense of these lines extending out in all directions, until they covered the entire world, the whole surface of the planet."

Eric fell silent. They were standing on the green of the eighth hole. The sun was edging down behind the western mountains, extending its shadow across the Las Vegas valley. The mountains on the eastern side were bathed in orange light by the last rays of the setting sun.

In their previous encounters the man had been a fountain of words, but so far this day Eric was doing most of the talking. He was not usually given to speaking spontaneously and at length, but today was different.

"That day in the park was the first time I had a sense about a direction for my life, something that I wanted to explore. I kept thinking about the heart, asking questions: When does the heart first begin beating? What tells it to beat? Why does it stop? I started to learn about the human body: the circulatory system, the nervous system, the muscles, cells, all the actions and interactions that are constantly going on inside us. It's incredible, it's really a miracle that all this activity is taking place inside us, automatically and continuously."

Eric felt a whirring noise shoot past his head, and a tiny green hummingbird hovered in front of him for a moment, then sped away.

"Did you know that a hummingbird's heart beats twelve hundred times a minute?" he asked.

The man smiled mischievously.

Eric was standing with his putter in his hands. He put it back into his bag and looked at the sky.

"We're losing the light. I think we just have time for one more hole."

The man nodded and said, "Yes, and then I think we should go from the ninth hole to the nineteenth," meaning the bar in the clubhouse.

Contrary to stereotype, Eric was not an avid golfer. His rented clubs felt awkward, and he was playing poorly. He didn't care; he was completely absorbed in his conversation with his partner. As they walked to the next tee, the man spoke.

"One thing to remember is, we are not just living on the planet Earth. We are a part of the Earth itself. We think we are living on a big ball that is so big we cannot know it, but we are part of the ball. All the things that are happening with the Earth also happen within us. Whether we know them or feel them or not, they are happening within us, things like, for example, thunder and lightning."

"You mean physically, within our bodies?" asked Eric.

"In a total sense," said the man, "in order to understand how thunder and lightning happen within us, we have to experience a very powerful part of nature: how it treats us. Then we will have a better sense about how thunder and lightning occur within us. Nature, or life, doesn't bring you into the world as a perfect baby. By nature, when you are born, you cry. There is no baby born with a belly laugh or a smile. That's a part of the innocence. We are all born imperfect. Our imperfect birth takes us into something very powerful. If you are born perfect your life will be very dull and boring. There will be nothing for you to do, nothing to grow into."

"But we *do* want to grow and perfect ourselves," Eric said, "is it just part of our nature to feel restless and unsatisfied?"

"First, you have to understand where you are. When the Buddha said the fundamental nature of life is suffering, he did not mean it as, 'Your life is painful.' What he said was like a password, a clue. He meant; your life is a struggle. You are struggling. Even if you have money and good relationships, still somehow in your life you are struggling. It just means that somehow or other you are experiencing a restlessness within you."

Eric nodded.

"You are restless, and it expresses itself in your life in various ways. You have mastered certain things, but still there is a restlessness. That restlessness is keeping you from experiencing something very powerful. It makes you feel there is something you are missing in your life, or something is not quite right with you. But what you feel is also a part of your own nature, the nature of your life. It can be said in one word: fear."

"It's not that right now you are emotionally frightened. Fear is not like a virus that is in your body. Fear, or whatever anxiety you feel, truly speaking, is a catalyst. It is a catalyst trying to get you to open the right windows in order to clean out the sounds that have settled and collected together in you, making you uneasy."

"By sounds, do you mean memories, internal dialogues?"

"Exactly. It's echoes, unfinished business, and it's making you very heavy and serious. When you can experience a lightness in your heart, that lightness comes out of whatever you are doing, if you are having fun with it. It doesn't matter what you are having fun with. You can have fun with your lover, your friends, even your thinking. Are you having fun with your thinking? Is thinking fun for you? Is feeling fun for you? Feeling as fun means surfing on the waves of your struggle. You can surf on the same waves that are now causing you to struggle, the waves of imperfection, impermanence and unpredictability."

"The waves are telling you this or that, and you are telling yourself, 'Oh, I can't believe what's happening to me,' 'No one understands me,' 'They don't get what I'm saying,' 'Nothing I'm doing is working out for me,' 'What's going on here? Is it the country? The politics?' No. It's not any of that. It is because you are not experiencing your space with thunder and lightning. When the space has thunder and lightning, there is something very powerful that comes to you."

"Okay," said Eric, "I know you're speaking metaphorically when you talk about thunder and lightning, but it sounds like a lot of turmoil and chaos inside oneself. Maybe I'm not understanding you."

"Right now, with or without your knowledge, you are trying to create a balance. You are trying to create a harmony, an evenness, some kind of stability. Those are all good, but the truth is, what you need is not just to be calm and cool. Most of the time, your calmness and coolness are artificial. You can sit in stillness, meditating, looking calm from the outside, but inside, emotionally, you are still masturbating, so it's not real. You look calm outside, but inside there are some volatile arguments going on. You are saying that something is bad."

"You are telling yourself your work is bad or people are bad, or your place is bad. There is always something you are saying to yourself, with or without your knowledge. What you need to have right now is a freshness. This freshness is a very powerful thunder that can come out of you. Thunder means a vibrancy. It's an incredible vibrancy you can feel without any specific goal or purpose or agenda."

"Do you mean that you feel great emotionally, regardless of your external circumstances?"

"Right now you have various goals and agendas for how you want to feel good. So, you have all kinds of thoughts, speculation, beliefs that are there: 'I need to do this or that, then I'll be okay.' You think you want this or that, and it makes you very serious. You achieved or received so many things, then years later you think, 'Wow, I thought that was what I wanted,' 'I thought this was the right girl,' 'I thought this was the right job.' They are all part of the imperfection, impermanence and unpredictability of life. You are trying to tell yourself certain things, telling yourself you are okay. Then you realize you are not okay, and you can laugh as well. It's like a punchline."

"A punchline?"

"You see, a joke works like this: first you have the set-up, the story, which tells you things are a certain way. Then you have the punchline, which pulls the rug from under you, tells you what you thought is not so. The thunder in the heart is a punchline without any words, without any statements or language at all. Without any kind of a build-up that says, 'This is it; this is how it is.' Thunder in the heart comes out of just pure love, pure transparency that we can experience through *non-resistance*. Silent, sweet surrender within ourselves."

Eric tried to restate what he had heard.

"The punchline is a wordless, emotional response to experience, a deeper appreciation of experience. And it comes out of realizing that things are *not* as you thought they were."

The man smiled.

"Thunder in the heart is like an emotional orgasm. In a normal physical or emotional orgasm, it is an infinite biological experience through your energies and through your emotions that connects you to another human being, or even by yourself—there are no rules about how you bring yourself into a climax, there is no harm. But in the emotional thunder it is an emotional orgasm in which you are bringing the circumference—the outer edge of your awareness—which seems ridiculously far away, or you think is impossible for you to touch, into the center core of your presence, where both of them collide together, and you experience the emission of an incredible energy called heart trust."

"What is heart trust?"

"Heart trust is the thunder in your heart, another way to say it. Thunder in the heart is an awareness, a knowing inside. It's a perception and an appreciation. It is pure. Pure means clear, uncontaminated, virgin. It's the sheer vibration of just being you. All the other things you are doing, with or without your knowledge, are manipulations. You don't think they're manipulations, 'No, I love her sincerely.' Those are the things we tell ourselves in order to have the various things we want."

"But thunder is a vibrancy, an emotional orgasm. You feel it in your body. It is not a knowledge or a realization. When it is in your body, you feel the incredible power of the universal energy around you. Right now, what you want to experience is the energy of friction, like in making love. Your pleasure and joy in life is a series of frictions that brings you into the excitement of fire, so your energy goes up. Which is fine, it is exciting. But all those pleasures are actually energies that are subject to impermanence."

"Right. Nothing lasts."

"Impermanence actually catches you pretty quickly. You are having a good time, then impermanence sees you. So you are looking at yourself in the mirror, and impermanence is like, 'Okay, what is he going to say now? I thought he was experiencing trust.' You go to the mirror and you get a shock because you don't look good. Who says you don't look good? It's just you. Do you have a loving kindness flowing out of your heart to the person, that innocent person in the mirror?"

"I never looked at myself like that. When I look in the mirror . . ."

"You immediately separate and become two people. The person in the mirror is looking at you, but you want to make sure you look good. So, your fingers are touching your hair, not the mirror. If loving kindness is coming out of you, then you will experience a vibrancy in the space between you and the mirror, as an incredible force of silence. You will be speechless, not because you can't talk, but because you'd rather not say a word because you are in the presence of a very powerful being who is looking at you."

"That sounds very powerful, and I'm sure it's a very real experience—for you. But honestly, to me, for me, it sounds very esoteric and hard to relate to. It sounds very—*exalted*. It's hard to believe I could feel something like that."

"Thunder is a vibrancy you feel, a condition of your presence. It is actually bringing your presence into a very powerful emotional energy. Thunder is emotional vitality, energy, intensity. It is a force waiting to stimulate and activate and awaken your energies—for what? So, you can go and investigate. You can pop up. That's what is waiting. And when it is right, then it will be followed by emotional lightning."

"Doesn't lightning come before thunder?"

"Always the thunder is followed by emotional lightning. When lightning happens, it is such a beautiful thing. It's a stimulus, it leaves us with awe. We get shocked by seeing lightning. It's a wave, it's an attraction, it's a transition, a shift. It leaves a trace for you to see clearly."

"Let me see if I understand. The thunder is an emotional resonance, from a full, a deeper experience of life, of my presence. And the lightning is being able to see life clearly, is that it?"

"That seeing clearly is actually part of your presence, feeling the incredible emotional love you have for you to just have fun. You cannot have fun without having your circumference in illumination. That circumference—the boundary of your awareness—has to be brightened, illuminated, radiant. You have to have such light in order to see. Right now, you are not clear. So, the lightning will reveal and unearth, unveil, and expose and disclose to you, make known to you, what the possibilities are that you have right now."

"That's exactly what I want."

"You have been going along with what you already know as possibilities, known data, known information. The lightning will erase all this information that you are holding unnecessarily. You are holding things, with or without your knowledge. You are holding things, emotionally and energetically. You should drop the whole thing. It's like eating a bad shrimp. It throws your system out of whack, not allowing you to enjoy what you are taking in right now."

"This emotional reflux keeps you from savoring new flavors, new loves. And now you are going to eat another bad shrimp. It looks better than the first shrimp you ate, but this guy is worse, this one is more crazy. It looks more appealing because you are hungry. Your hunger is a compulsion, not a passion."

"Okay, So just as we might have undigested food that's upsetting us, we have old thoughts, feelings, beliefs, that are polluting our ability to enjoy life. Is that a fair restatement?"

"When your hunger is a not a passion, but a compulsion, you are not able to get into the right flow of life. This is very important to understand. The thunder comes and unleashes the lightning. Thunder means focus. When you are totally focused, your energy is so condensed that you have no past or present. You are in focus, you are completely clear, sharp, centered. You have a focal point. You have a heart; you have a core. Now you can concentrate. Now, out of this focus comes the thunder. It's a sound. The sound is not words. You don't have any echo. When you have thunder, all the background sounds disappear. All the inner dialogues and the background sounds disappear, and then your focus is direct and clear, your energy is very clear, so that now you can sense and feel and appreciate the true nature of your heart, which is pure and innocent."

"I don't feel pure and innocent."

"You have told yourself that you are not pure and innocent, based on your track record. Nature doesn't bring you to the world as a perfect baby, understand. It brings you into the world with imperfection, unpredictability, and impermanence, for you to savor the spice of life. They are the emotional flavors. These emotional flavors are there for you to feel and acknowledge. They come as a game of brilliance, which, if you can pay attention, will open a very different luminosity and light to you, to bring about the right energy in you."

"How do I connect to that?"

"The thunder in the heart will come if you don't interfere. Don't interfere with your heart that is always trying to open into freedom. The heart is always rising. It never stops. The heart is always in a vertical ascendance, illuminating rays of discovery. Putting brilliant rays of discovery, giving awareness of your true energy as a lion, meaning fearlessness. And involving you in games of— not chance—of evolution."

"What do you mean by 'games of evolution'?"

"You are right now, without your knowledge, engaging in games of chance. Those games of chance are a trick by infinite intelligence, cloaking your understanding of the imperfection, the impermanence, and the unpredictability. They are games going through your mind. These are not the games you play with other people, or in the stock market, or in the casino. These are games you play with yourself. You are calculating the risk of doing something with somebody, or you are calculating and deciding whether to go here or there. Your calculations are going to trap you, because the only reason you are calculating is because something within you is not clean and clear."

"What you called porous and transparent?"

"If you are clean and clear, you go out and play with anyone, a man or a woman, an invention or a discovery, fearlessly, because it will give you an insight, a perception, and an appreciation, because you love what you are doing. So, the thunder in the heart always tells you to go with your energy. Never ever say bad things to yourself. Go with your energy and the thunder and the lightning will open the transparency within you. The whole idea is for you to become an absolutely pure being. It means transparency, yes, a porousness, not holding onto anything."

"Your skin is porous. You don't know that; you don't see it. In the same way, your emotional body has various colors all over, various impurities. If you are totally transparent, cool air can go through you. It's not just cool air that will go through you. What will go through you are the forces of the elements, enabling you to recognize them around you as energies, ideas, brilliance and connections."

"What do you mean by the 'forces of the elements'?"

"Right now, you have the pleasure of gravity just holding you and carrying you without your knowledge, making all your body functions effortless. It never says, 'You have to exercise, you have to go to sleep, you have to wake up.' No, it says, 'Don't worry, I will give all that to you, you just play.' Play with what? Play with your heart openings, by discovering new emotions, new ideas. Making new connections. Most of the connections you have with people now are boring. You go along with them because you don't know what else to do. Nature doesn't want you to just go along, go to sleep, and die. Nature says you are here to have fun."

"Thunder in the heart is fun?"

"Thunder is the vibrancy of an emotional orgasm. Feel it without giving yourself statements. When was the last time you were not talking to yourself? When was the last time you experienced a sense of vibrancy that was so powerful you didn't have a single thought? If you don't have a single thought, you don't have a measurement of time. If you have no thoughts, you have no time. One day you may actually experience that."

"Why can't I experience that right now?"

"Right now, you are just unearthing yourself, discovering yourself. What I am doing is disrobing you, in order to bring to light the truth about you. The truth about you is, you are a magical child, full of innocence, sweetness, and wonder. Magic is the nature of the fun of life. You are thrilled by whatever appears and disappears. Not the magic of a Vegas show. What appears and disappears creates a wave, that's why you are excited. You are excited to catch the wave, not to catch somebody disappearing through a hat or a coffin in a magic show. That is illusion."

"But what you have to see is the appearance and disappearance of the waves of emotion in front of you, where doubt becomes truth, or fear becomes love. They are coming out of you and you are not able to experience the flavors of them, because your mind is too busy. Busy finding money, sex and power. Your gut level says, 'That's all very good, but I have to find money. I have to eat. I need to find money.' And then the area below the gut level says, 'I have a little money, I have to find sex, I need to find intimacy.' And then the heart says, 'I have a little bit of those other two things I want, but I am not secure.'"

"All those things are just illusions. Those are all part of the illusion that you are going with. What you need to do is to bring yourself to life as somebody incredibly fresh and new. You *are* fresh and new, because you are born today. You woke up today into an incredible freshness and thunder in your emotional heart. When you get up, what you feel is very clear, uncontaminated. Whenever you wake up you are a virgin boy or girl. Just feel that, it's a sheer vibrancy."

"Life is fascinating because it brings you light to illuminate. What is the light you need? You need emotional clarity. That's all you need to reveal, unearth, and discover the new feelings you have. They have new words, they may have new colors, they may have new openings. Around you is a space. That space is open, even right now, waiting for you to come and feel. And you are able to sense with your whole heart, your whole body, that life is good because you are here. It's not that life is good, and you are here. It's not that you are here in a good life. No. Life is good *because you are here*. Your presence is here. Life is telling you, 'Thank you for being here.'"

"That's very beautiful."

"And your presence also activates a connection to a greater circle, called humanity. Humanity is a greater circle, a huge orchestra made of kindness, compassion, consideration, tenderness, generosity, sensitivity, love, determination, will, guts, spirit. That's the circle you have. That is the circle that allows you to experience your being here with energy and with vigor."

"That's even more beautiful. It makes me realize that my feelings toward humanity have always been somewhat fearful and defensive."

"All the things you have experienced are coming out of a balance that you thought you needed. Coming out of trying to make your life symmetrical and harmonious. But now you are experiencing a new sound of music. That music is the thunder in your heart. Thunder in your heart means sensing around you an incredible vibrancy that you have, so that you can love. Love becomes your search. It's not the search for intelligence or the manifestation of goodness. Love is the search for who you are. Not your memory. Not the path you have traveled so far. Love is the search that will thrill you about who you are. Not your history or ancestry. They are all great, but they are gone. Now you are here."

"Now I am here."

Eric felt an odd sensation, like prickly heat, when he said the words.

"Now *I* am here," he said again, "and I have something to contribute to the life of my time. Just as much to contribute as anyone else. I feel that inside, but I never let myself believe it."

The man smiled.

"People came to the Earth in different circles, everybody who has been born. Most of the people are what I call 'survivors.' They just live their life and die, and new people are born, and that's part of the cycle. And then there are others who came. They were fascinated by the presentation of life. They were discoverers, scientists, they became great kings or incredible human beings who built up the human race into the experience of pure wonder."

Eric nodded his head.

"And then there are a few other people, like the Buddha, Christ, Krishna, and others. They come from what I call a circle of liberation. They found ways to release people who are struggling and bring happiness to people's hearts. And now, there is something very special happening."

"What do you mean?"

"I'm talking about where we are right now in the world. Once in a while, the elements send an incredible signal, and people feel it, like a cool breeze, or an actual organic touch. The last time on Earth that it happened was in the 1960s. When this wave of coolness entered then, all over the world people suddenly started to feel free. People began to make love, not for marriage, but just loving each other. The flower children were born, the Beatles, marijuana, all those things. It became a period of questioning, exploring. And then it disappeared."

"The last time it came to Earth before the 1960s was in Jesus's time, about two thousand years back. Earlier, it was in Krishna's and Buddha's times. And then it disappeared. I have a sense that the earth is again opening that space. But remember, when it opens the space, not only do people become very brilliant, compassionate, and loving. Even in those days there were wars. There were wars alongside the incredible realizations and brilliance that some people went through. They happen together. It's like a sweet and sour dish."

"And you feel that we're coming to another period like that? The sixties were not that long ago. Isn't that a very short period for that kind of historical cycle to repeat itself?"

"When you think about what happened in the 1960s, not only did people have unconditional love and sex and marijuana and all those things—the chemistry changed within their bodies. They became different. Now their babies have had babies. And the second and third generations are beginning to have a little awareness about it. But this is only for a few thousand people in the world, who will be able to transcend into spaces where whatever you are struggling with will disappear."

"How does that happen?"

"In order to do that, you have to come out with a very clear awareness. Right now, what is the struggle that you are experiencing? What are you struggling with right now? It may look like you are fine, you are great, but still you have a certain struggle within you. You have to catch it, discover and find out and unearth it. That can develop and evolve for you to have a new energy. And with a new energy, you are looking into a new world, right now, with you."

Around the two men the twilight was deepening. Soon the first stars would appear. The world felt still and silent to Eric. It *did* feel like a new energy and a new world. Across the Las Vegas strip, the powerful light atop the Luxor hotel, the brightest single light source in the world, projected straight up into the sky.

"What happens is, normally in our aging process we come out with new ideas, new excitements and fascinations, but the body cannot take it. Your body cannot take it. So, what the greatest scientists and Buddha and others did was, they created a lightness, an illumination, a fluorescence, a shaft of light in your body that becomes porousness, transparency. So you begin to sense and feel things that you are not able to experience right now."

"So then, your sensitivity, your appreciation, your compassion and tenderness will explode. Once that explodes, your presence will have a different sense of space, an opening and a vastness. Normally we don't feel a sense of vastness within us, we feel a vastness *around* us. So, this is what I am bringing to you now: to uncover and reveal a different intelligence that will stimulate you. Not the intelligence you know right now, for survival. It's a different intelligence, that comes in like lightning, so that you can feel around you and see around you, and that will be an emotional stimulus and a transmission that can create an incredible focus in your life."

"You are good, you're fine, and you should feel very good, but this is a different life right now. It has to evolve. Feeling good has to evolve. You can't be just feeling good, because then the body begins to slowly contract. Your body is made out of sound. All of the energies of the body are sounds. It's like a tone, a reverberation. For you to communicate and articulate your brilliance, you need a different sound, you need a little more tuning. That will open you to be fascinated by things you are not yet experiencing. And that's the sound that will come out and will open you into the real thunder of life."

"You make it sound so easy. And fun. I always tended to think that great discoveries and breakthroughs were the product of superhuman efforts that honestly, I never felt myself capable of. And you seem to be telling me that I just need to be sensitive and have fun."

"You can't believe actually that life loves you so much. Life loves your presence here. And because of that there is the beautiful thunder, the deepest vibrancy that you have. It is an orgasm without sex. It is an orgasm without making love, just being you. It's an awareness and appreciation that brings you to life, to reveal and unveil, unearth and discover that it happened to be *you* who is you."

"That is the contribution that the Earth gives to you, and in return you are saluting. And your salute is in your fingertips, and you are standing always at the tip of the Earth. Wherever you are right now is the tip of the Earth, in which you are experiencing the evenness and the stability, the command and the authority. You are not actually the commander of the universe. You are better than that. You are the commander of the whole infinite space, with your heart opening your presence, illuminating with a song."

Standing at the center of the green, he stretched out his arms, threw back his head and sang, "I know that you know that I love you! What I want you to know is that I know that you love me!"

CHAPTER 7

THE CHEMISTRY OF WINNING

"This is the biggest provocation in life: for you to predict the unpredictable, predict the impermanent, and predict the imperfect."

Mark was floating on his back, the blue sky filling his field of vision. A few white clouds drifted here and there, and in the periphery of his vision he saw the tops of the hotel's towers. The pool area was not thronged with people, as it was in the summer months, and there was enough room for him to spread his limbs wide and float freely in the sunlight. He had spent the morning in the casino and the afternoon in the spa. He had arranged to meet the man—Mark thought of him as Mr. 'Aha!'—at the spa, and after massage, steam and sauna, they adjourned to the pool area.

Mark moved his arms gently in the water and drifted slowly to the edge of the pool. He rolled over and pulled himself out of the water. The sunshine was warm, but a sudden breeze chilled him. He wrapped a towel around his shoulders and walked quickly back to his cabana, where the man sat in the shade, sipping iced tea. Mark sat down, drank the last of his iced tea, and ordered a mojito.

"I had a great time in the casino today. I took your advice: before I did any betting, I just watched. I was watching the roulette table for a long time, just watching which numbers were hitting, which colors, how many odds, how many evens. It's really interesting—when I wasn't betting, I was much more aware of overall patterns. At one point, I noticed that it had landed on four numbers in line with each other—not in numerical order, but next to each other on the table layout. First 29, then 26, then 23, and then 20 – right up the center of the table! So, I put a bet on 17."

"And did it win?"

"No!" Mark laughed, "No, it didn't! So, much for the 'flow'!"

The man laughed.

"That wasn't the flow, that was you thinking you knew something, doing some very clever guessing. Actually, there doesn't have to be any kind of pattern of reason why a certain number will come up. You will see it coming, and you should not ask why—that will only bring your mind back into it."

Mark grimaced.

"It's pretty hard to tell sometimes, whether it's the flow, or just wishful thinking, eh?"

"Here is one way to tell: did you put all your money on your bet, on 17?"

"No, I made a small bet, just in case."

"If you had really felt it, you would have put all your money on it, because there would be no doubt."

"You're killing me! But anyway, I did have a good time, and I did pretty well. I played a lot of blackjack. First, I watched. I played at four different tables. As soon as I started to go down, I pulled out and went somewhere else. I remembered what you said about it being fun. I have a tendency to take things personally. I get mad at the dealer or the table, and I want to get even, and I end up screwing myself."

"That's very good," said the man, "It is, truly, not personal, and anyway, having fun is the best revenge."

"I love it!" said Mark.

"How are you feeling about the other thing, about your wife?"

"Well, now that I think about it, it's actually kind of the same principle as the gambling. I've been feeling guilty, for a long time, feeling like I fucked up, like it's a personal failure on my part, and at the same time I'm angry and resentful about having to change. But maybe I need to step away from the table for a minute, so to speak. Just watch the game from a distance for a little while, do you know what I mean?"

"That's brilliant," said the man, "You're a smart guy. You're able to see it this way because you already have a feeling for seeing life as a game. It comes naturally to you, but it's not fully conscious in you. I'm going to bring it out for you to really feel it."

"Well, thank you very much!" said Mark with a hearty laugh, "I don't know why you're doing all this for me, but I'll take it! And, just to say thank you, tonight I'm going to buy you the best dinner you ever had."

"Oh, thank you so much, but I'm afraid I can't make it tonight. Can we do it tomorrow?"

"Got a date? Okay, man of mystery, tomorrow it is."

"Great. Always remember, life is a game, no matter how heavy or serious it seems. Whether it is your job, or relationships, or anything, life is a game and we play to win. We are born. Why are we born? We are born to play. That's why we are born. And whatever we call our play, whether it is playing soccer, playing chess, playing volleyball, or playing roulette or card games—they are all games. And these are not the only games we play. We play emotional games with each other. We play a lot of games with each other."

"Oh yeah," said Mark dolefully.

"But in every game, there is one excitement. You play a game to win. You don't play for a draw. You always play a game to win. So, in your game of life, are you winning right now? Or are you losing? Or are you at a draw? Where are you? This is very important to understand. Life is absolutely a game. And whatever you call it, whether you are working with computers, with buildings, with chemistry, with food or other things, all that you are doing is actually also play."

"Do you feel playful? Are you enjoying what you are doing? Or are you serious and heavy with what you are doing? If you are serious and heavy with what you are doing, you are not playing. Then you will become a story-maker. All the stories, one way or the other, however real they may appear, are fictitious. It's fiction. We can make a whole story about 'What is the Cosmos?' 'What is God?' 'What is Awakening?' or 'How to Win at Blackjack,' all these things. There is no such thing as 'How to Win.'"

"No? Isn't that what you've been telling me—how to win?"

"Number one thing to understand in the game of life, or the game of roulette, or the game of chess, or the stock market—it's not actually how to win. It's more than how to win."

"You think you are in the game. But most of the time, you are *out* of the game. You are just a witness; you are just an observer. You are just looking at somebody else's game or something else. You are yelling 'Hooray!' at the basketball players or football players. You are just a cheerleader. And most of the time, you are not actually a great cheerleader, because you are distracted. You are distracted by the other cheerleaders' costumes and how they look, or what the players are saying and doing. There are a lot of mind attacks going through you."

"Whenever you are playing, are you at ease, with a sense of highly-charged excitement? Or are you feverish? If you are feverish, you should actually be taking a shower or going to bed. You should not be playing any games at all."

"In any game there are—not exactly rules—there are instructions for how to play the game. Number one is, you should love what you are going to play. If you are not going to love what you are playing—don't play it. Don't play the game. You should *love* what you are going to play. And while your intention is to win, your intention should not be how much you get out of winning. It's not about the end result of how much. You should have the *love* to play. The love to play is your key. It is the key that allows you to make the right next move. In all play there is one thing. Whether you are playing a chess game or baccarat, or roulette, or playing a tennis game—any game—it's called *the next move*."

"What is your next move? What is your next vision? What are you able to see? This is very important. That is how you can defeat even a grand master in chess who knows all the moves. You may be an amateur, or you may be brilliant, but if you can see a couple of moves ahead because you are not stuck in time—if you can see that way, without time, in the game, then you are actually winning. In that winning, it's not a fever, it's a surrender.

"Any winning should make you humble, make you appreciate. It's not just an ego boost. You can boost your ego after you go home and have a drink!"

Mark raised his glass and laughed.

"It's easy for me to understand what it means to treat life as a game. I get that. And I understand that treating life as a game doesn't mean that you're frivolous or dishonest. Just the opposite. I feel like you're teaching me to have more fun and be more serious, both at the same time. But when you talk about things like being stuck in time, I've got to say, you lose me. Is it really possible for me to be sensitive enough to feel these things you're describing? How do I do that?"

"You have to be in a space of non-interference. Inside that circle, you are not getting interference from three things. Number one, from your mind attacks, which come to you as unpredictability. Number two, from distractions, which challenge your focus, patience and fascination. And number three, from distortions, which are the most common, and which come when you tell yourself a story about how your life sucks."

"But my life *does* suck!" said Mark with a laugh.

"Your mind should not be talking to you and telling you, 'Okay, do this, do that.' Your mind is always calculating. Don't listen to your mind. When your mind is shut off, there is a blue light that comes. That's called your heart drive. Your heart drive is your fascination for discovery. Fascination for discovery is a blue fire that comes out of you. In your fascination for discovery, you are having an emotional erection."

"Whoa!" interjected Mark.

The man went on.

"You are having an emotional ascendance. You are emotionally aroused, but you don't just jump and make love. If you are a great lover, no matter how excited you are, you're *gentle*. It's gently entering into another person, another space. You have to be gentle. If there is any feverishness, still you can enter, but you may not be totally there. You have to be in a space of *absolute grace*."

"Grace?"

"Grace doesn't mean anything spiritual. Very simply, grace means *at ease*. Grace means you are cool with yourself. Even if you know the next pull of the lever will win the Megabucks. If you know with certainty that the next pull of the Megabucks lever will win you $300 million—be cool. Sit on the chair, stretch out your hands, crack your knuckles, yawn. When the waiter goes by, tip him all your cash. Why? Because you don't have to worry. With the next move, you will be winning the lottery. Then, just hold your hand on the lever, with your friends all around you— and you know the next move is going to change your whole life. Take your hand away again! Don't be in a rush. Just feel the grace. Feel what is life, the exuberance of the life force, the life energy that made your human body, that made your human heart. You have gone through all these things in your life, but in the next second your life is going to change, so take it easy. Don't be in a hurry! In fact, if you want to, clap your hands, make your friends feel that you are going crazy, nuts! It doesn't matter what they are thinking. Hold the lever, and you don't have to keep your eyes open—why?—because you are *sure*. When you are 100% sure, close your eyes, then put your hand, and very slowly, slowly, slowly pull the lever towards you. And then you will hear the most unbelievable sound of everybody cheering—keep your eyes closed! Pretend like you can't open your eyes, then, slowly open them. Your life has changed. That's how you win, my friend."

Mark had been on the edge of his seat, and now he applauded.

"Bravo! That was beautiful. That's the eternal dream, isn't it? Just to *know*. To absolutely *know* what's coming."

"Part of the thing to understand is that gambling existed throughout human history. People gambled. They didn't call it gambling, but they did it. They did various things to trade or barter, and they had superstitions, they are all part of gambling. And now, in the twenty-first century, the electronic age, everything is so fast, so quickly changing. The thing about this age is change is instant. But though the change is instant, there is something we have to remember — whether you call it the stock market, or you are playing roulette, or baccarat—you are playing in order to win. You are playing to win. You don't play to lose, but most of the people, they lose. They lose their money, they lose their family, everything."

Mark said, "That's true, most of the time, you lose. Gambling isn't a good bet, so to speak. So, why do people love it so much?"

"So, this is something we really have to understand. We play any game to win, but there is more to it than just winning. If the art of the game is just winning, then there will be no gaming. There is something very fascinating to understand about the nature of the game. The game is inviting you to *catch* something, like you are a hunter. You have to target the right one. You can't shoot all the birds to get the right one. You have to shoot only the right bird. In the game, you can't just go everywhere, all over the place. It is asking you to connect, or to discover, or to win a bet. Whether the bet is the stock market, or picking the winning lottery numbers, or playing against the house in baccarat, it's winning."

"So, you have to forget about winning in order to win? It's hard for me to get my mind around that."

"What is actually happening with your mind right now? Your mind is based on one word: order. The language of the mind is order. The mind doesn't contain chaos. Chaos cannot be comprehended by the mind. The nature of life is, however, a flow. The nature of life that we experience every day in our emotions, in our thinking, in our feelings—or in a gaming situation, whether baccarat or whatever—it's a flow. What is the flow made out of? The flow is made out of the same three basic fundamental waves that life contains. That is, imperfection, impermanence, and unpredictability. That's the same thing that is going through a pack of cards, or the stock market, whatever it is you are dealing with. The flow is imperfect. The flow is impermanent. And the flow is unpredictable."

"There are those words again. But seriously, how can the flow be imperfect? It just is what it is, isn't it?"

"When I say the flow is imperfect, what does 'imperfect' mean? It's very important to understand. It doesn't have a perfect pattern. It doesn't have a symmetrical order. For example, if the number eight comes up four times in a row, your mind says the fifth time it will not be the number eight. But not only is it possible for it to come up a fifth time, but it is actually the very natural flow of imperfection to reappear again."

"The flow is imperfect, and the flow is impermanent—that means, very simply, *you can't hold it.* You can't hold onto the ball when somebody throws it to you. You can hold it for just a moment, then you have to throw it somewhere else. Otherwise, someone will come and tackle you and grab the ball. So, that's what impermanence means, only momentarily can you see it, then it will change."

"And the flow is unpredictable," Mark put in, "that seems pretty obvious, right?"

"What unpredictability means— it's very strange. Unpredictability means the same number may repeat even fourteen times, breaking all the odds. You say, 'Oh, no, that's impossible.' I have seen that happen. A number came fourteen times! One number, it was red nineteen, came fourteen times, and I think that was the world record. That is very rare, but a very rare occurrence is still possible."

Something dawned on Mark. His eyes widened.

"There's no pattern or order in the flow. Sooo there's no way the mind can predict it, right? So, if I'm going to actually get what you're saying, actually be able to feel it, put it in practice, I've got to leave my *mind behind.*"

"What I'm trying to show here is how you can get into the flow, so you can predict the unpredictable. If you can do that, you are a winner. This is the biggest provocation in life: for you to predict the unpredictable, predict the impermanent, and predict the imperfect. Those three."

"You heard what I said, right? Mind behind? I thought that was pretty clever."

The man smiled indulgently.

"When you think about your mind, how many times did you change today, from morning till right now? Right now, what you feel is not what you felt in the morning. Your thoughts change, your feelings change. You were upset, you were happy, you were excited, you were sad, you were agitated, you were weird, you were great, you were wonderful, you were in fascination, confusion, you were in appreciation, you were in anger. How many times did you change? It's not for you to think about that and feel pissed off and get worried about it. Be *fascinated* by it."

"I go back and forth with you," Mark said, "because sometimes you describe things, and they seem incredibly complicated, or subtle, and other times you tell me something and it's so simple, like 'be fascinated,' and I don't know how to deal with that, either."

"The first lesson of knowing how to win in life is: be fascinated by the presentation of imperfection. Be fascinated by the presentation of unpredictability. Be fascinated by the presentation of impermanence. Those are very powerful. You have to be fascinated. When you are fascinated by these things, then your energy changes. If you are in fascination, you are ready. Because when you are in fascination, you are cool. What does cool mean? You are transparent. What is meant by transparent? You are like a hollow bamboo. If you are not a hollow bamboo, never make a bet. If you are not transparent, in fascination, never gamble, whether it is in the stock market, gaming, it doesn't matter, never make any bet. Never."

"Your mind is telling you all these things; your mind is feverish. Your fever doesn't come from your heart. It comes from your gut level. At your gut level, you have so much undigested bullshit, undigested emotions, energies. And that is what's driving you crazy. You have to be cool."

"Understand this. Feel this. It's very important you feel and understand this. Your gut level has to be so clear. If you want to make any stock market bets or play roulette or gamble—there's nothing *wrong* about it. But you have to be cool and clear."

"Now keep in mind," said Mark, "that I need very simple answers, but tell me, how do I get my gut level clear of undigested bullshit?"

"Please drink a whole cup of very hot water before you go anywhere to make any bet. Get a cup of hot water and sit somewhere for no reason. Put your right palm over your left one, with your two thumbs placed together. Be cool, and breathe deeply. Your mind is going to go crazy, thinking about what you are going to do with the stock market, how you are going to gamble with your money, and also you may have fantasies about what you are going to do. You are going to be in mental masturbation about the end result. All of that is okay. But prepare yourself for how you can connect to the flow. You have to empty yourself, empty your story, empty your mind. You have to empty everything. And then only are you ready to play, ready to win."

"It doesn't matter whether you are playing a chess game, whether you are playing baccarat, whether you are playing roulette or the stock market – be at ease. And never play with alcohol. You believe you can think better with alcohol. No, you can never think better with alcohol. You get distorted."

"Never alcohol?"

"Drink hot water, almost steaming hot, a whole cup. Not coffee, not scotch, not orange juice—hot water. And you have to sit on a chair and put your right palm into your left palm with thumbs touching and just breathe deeply and very gently tap the two thumbs only, very deeply touch the two thumbs together. The fingers are never intertwined or crossed; they are loose. And breathe deeply."

"I will tell you right now, the moment you try to do that, thoughts will come, fantasies will come, the mind will come. It's okay, you're just not used to having emptiness, you are not used to being totally free. You are not used to having a moment of your life without any thoughts. But don't worry, it doesn't mean you are doing something wrong. It's just that you aren't used to it."

"No, I'm not used to it at all."

"I am cultivating a new space in you. I am bringing a new space into your heart, into your being. So, this is a new lens through which you can see through time and space, you can see the flow. When you are doing the stock market or gambling, you will not be feverish, you will be cool and excited. This is what I am bringing to you. I am bringing a coolness, and a fire in your heart to do this. This is a win-win situation. This is what you need to do. This is what it is."

"Do this practice, not actually at the place, but before you go to any casino, or play the stock market, or anywhere you want to go. You do this practice at home. Then, when you are going to wherever it is you want to go, get into the car, and just sit there, coolly. Don't be in a rush, driving fast to play fast. You have to be cool and at ease. When you get into the car, touch the rim of the steering wheel with love. Put your fingertips at the top and bring them down a few times. Touch the wheel with love."

"I like that," said Mark, "I've got a very nice car, and I should definitely show her some love."

"Understand, the very nature of play is actually *fascination*. It's not about winning."

"Stop right there," said Mark, "how can you say it's not about winning? You've been telling me that I should always play to win."

"The nature of the play is fascination and excitement for you to see the flow. Your fascination is your ability to predict the flow. Because the game is telling you you can't predict. Whether it is the stock market or gambling, all the games are telling you one thing: 'Catch me if you can!' They are telling you, 'Catch me,' because they are able to change at any time, moment by moment. But you are faster than time. How can you be faster than time? Only if you are not living in time right now."

"There you go again. What is 'living in time'?"

"How you live in time is by scheming and planning, fantasizing and thinking, speculating and guessing. From now on, you are never going to guess. You are not going to make decisions based on guessing."

"How do I stop guessing?"

"What we are doing, with or without our knowledge, is we are holding so many things. Holding our emotions, holding our thoughts. We are holding grudges, we are holding diffused anger, we are holding resentment, so many things. And that holding has made you one thing: *serious*. Heavy. And whatever you are holding creates another thing: it creates a shadow. Because when you are holding something, you are not actually *transparent*. The moment you are not transparent, when the light is not going through you, you will always have a shadow. The shadow is what you get frightened by. Your own shadow frightens you. Your own darkness frightens you. It makes you doubtful, you become fearful. When you are in darkness and fearful, never, ever play—whether the stock market or chess or gambling."

"So, I need to be very selective about when I play? Be very sensitive to when is the right time?"

"Never play if you are in a state of anxiety. You can be one hundred percent sure that you will fail. You think you can change the fear into anger and then crush your opponent. No, you can never do that. Because whatever the darkness, no matter how little or heavy it is, light is stronger. Light is love, light is fascination, light is winning. So understand, if you have any darkness, never play."

"Got it. Darkness, never play. What else?"

"If you are going to play the stock market, if you are going to do any kind of gambling, before you do that, I suggest you take a shower. Take a very hot shower and end it with very cool water. Rotate your hands in front of, and away from, your body, making any sound. It looks like a crazy thing to do, but that will unleash you, make you free. It will charge you with energy, releasing whatever you are holding. Do that and you will be in good shape."

"I like these exercises you give me to do. I like having something concrete to do, instead of mentally trying to grasp everything you're saying. I can see the logic of those exercises – the one with the mirror, the hot water – they're disciplines to make me more aware, to change my routine behaviors. Hey, are you going to charge me for this?"

They laughed.

"You have to be in good shape to play. Not physically — you have to be *empty*. When you are empty, you are playing with the infinite intelligence. Understand this. You are not just playing with cards; you are not just playing with stocks. That's the way it appears. Whatever the game you are playing, you are connecting to a flow. You are about to *predict* something. You are about to predict a change in the flow."

"A change in the flow—you mean, like what number is coming up?"

"What is meant by predicting the flow is, you are predicting the future. You are predicting the next moment. That's how every game works. If it's the stock market—predicting what will happen with Apple, what will happen with Starbucks—you are able to *see* that and *feel* it, if you are in a timeless space. If you are in any darkness or shadow, you can't do that. Predicting the flow comes when you are empty."

"Empty, meaning no undigested bullshit?"

"Emptiness is also a very powerful way you can feel your *innocence*. Innocence means you are like a baby. If you really want to hit the target, you need to have a baby-like innocence, a baby-like playfulness. A magical energy comes out of that."

Mark stood up, drained his glass and did a little shadow boxing on the wall of the cabana.

"As soon as I get dressed, I'm going back to the casino. You're making me feel like I'm seeing something out of the corner of my eye, and I can't quite pin it down. At the very least, you're making me excited to play. I don't understand a lot of what you say, but I understand what you're telling me to do: be more sensitive. Don't be feverish. Don't be heavy."

The man smiled and nodded.

"All the shadows are connected to one energy: gravity. You can't predict anything with the speed of gravity. The only time you predict and it comes true is at the *speed of light*. The speed of light—like a flash, you see it, you realize, you recognize, you acknowledge, you are in fascination, you are in focus—then you hit the target—boom! You hit it and you win the game."

CHAPTER 8

THE POWER OF BEING YOU

"You are here, right now, in the present moment, facing infinite intelligence."

The first day of the conference had gone smoothly for Eric. In the morning he had attended a panel discussion on new medical devices and their applications, checked the status of the day's other events, had lunch with three of his colleagues, and then went back to his room to work on his presentation. Once the conference was underway and moving forward as planned, a great deal of Eric's anxiety had eased. Nothing disastrous had happened, and the attendees generally seemed happy and excited.

As Eric's anxiety about the conference receded, however, his anxiety about his own contribution moved to the foreground. He had a talk prepared. All he had to do was get up and deliver it, but there was something else he very much wanted to say, something he felt compelled to say, that he had not yet put into words.

Something completely unexpected had happened to Eric already during this trip. Two things, in fact. His meeting Mark on the plane had reminded him of a time in his life before a series of choices had locked him into a path that now seemed rigid and narrow. And then, the talkative stranger had knocked him completely off-balance and left him teetering between excitement and terror, as if he were on a rope bridge over an abyss.

He had struggled all afternoon with the text of his presentation, and while he now had a clearer idea of what he wanted to say, the thought of saying it filled him with dread.

It was now after seven, and Eric had come down to the casino looking for the man. The previous night, on the golf course, the man had mentioned that he enjoyed baccarat, and that Eric could probably find him there. Eric was not sure what baccarat was, and he was exploring the casino looking for it. As he wandered, he noted all the different and varied games. There were rows upon rows of flashing and chiming slot machines. He jumped a bit when a machine chirped, "Yoo-hoo!" as he passed. He looked into the poker room, where stoic men in dark glasses guarded their cards. Packs of rowdy young men strolled in the aisles, ogling gaggles of young women. He saw games he didn't know, like Pai Gow and Texas Hold 'em, and those he recognized, like craps, roulette and blackjack. Eventually, he found the baccarat room, and passed through its arches into relative quiet. The man was seated at a table across the room, his back to Eric.

Eric looked around the room. The players all seemed to be moving very slowly, as if they had all the time in the world. Eric moved across the room, feeling extremely awkward and out of place as he approached the man's table. This man had been so generous with his time and his attention, as if he and Eric were old friends, yet they were complete strangers. How much more of the man's time could Eric presume upon? He looked so relaxed and contented at the table, surely he had no more time for Eric's dithering? Eric was on the verge of retreating, when the dealer addressed him.

"Sir?"

"Oh, no, I was just . . ." he stammered, and the man turned around.

"Heyyy," he said warmly, "Good to see you. Let me just finish up here and we'll go and eat. Why don't you go and have a drink and I'll meet you at the steakhouse, okay?"

"That would be great!" Eric blurted gratefully.

Twenty minutes later, he was seated in a booth in the hotel's elegant steakhouse. A glass of scotch was warming him inside, and his nerves were giving way to relaxation and anticipation. Soon he saw the man enter and the host greeted him effusively. 'Does he know *everybody*?' Eric thought. The host gestured in his direction and the man smiled and waved. He spoke to the bartender, then joined Eric in his dark, wood-paneled booth.

"How is your project going?" he asked.

"I'm going to make a fool of myself!"

Eric surprised himself with the intensity of his reply, but kept on speaking.

"I want to share something, the things I was telling you on the golf course. I've been practicing a very mechanistic type of medicine, but there are things going on at subtler levels that could be profoundly important. I have an intuition about it, nothing definite. And that's not critical at this point. What I want to communicate is the feeling of magic, the excitement of exploring new territory—that's what leads to innovation and discovery. I know you understand what I'm talking about, but will anyone else? Who do I think I am, to think anyone should be impressed by this? A conference like this is for sharing information, not emotional ranting!"

The man was smiling. The waiter appeared and set a glass of scotch in front of him.

He fixed his gaze on Eric.

"You are going to do something incredible," he said, "something only you can do. And for that, you need guts, you need fire, and you have it. Your life has been going in a certain track, and it's great, but now is the time for you to really come out, and sing a song, and you're the only one who can make that song."

"It's not just this speech" Eric said, "That's a big thing—a terrifying thing, frankly—but my whole life is at a crossroads. I have a very solid life, very good. I have a wife and three kids, who I love very much, there's no problem there—and two cars and a house and an office that I share with my partners, and certifications, subscriptions, licenses, payments, schedules, policies— there's an incredible paranoia about lawsuits—all this stuff I support and maintain by being completely dependable and predictable and by, in a certain way, turning myself off, and always staying within certain bounds. It's not like I want to go crazy and run away or anything like that, but isn't there some way I can *express* myself more, make what I'm doing more fascinating, more of an exploration, more *fun*?"

"The most incredible thing in life," said the man, "is that it is you who happened to be you. Your life was given to you, and you have, always, complete freedom and choice, to do anything you wish."

He took a sip of scotch.

"The power of being you is something which is lying dormant most of the time. It doesn't really have a passage to truly come out. It's not about understanding who you are. You are alive. You are here in the world, you have a human body, you have a heart, you have feelings, you have thoughts and energy, and you are here to have a good time. Everything else is secondary, whether you call it obligations, duties—they are not true at all. You are making them up. You are making them up because you feel somehow unworthy, not good enough."

"I'm not making up my obligations, believe me."

"You are making up all kinds of stories to confirm that you are no good, and that you will remain that way. I am trying to break the chains of the network that is holding you prisoner inside, keeping you from creating fantastic pleasure and joy in living."

There were moments with the man when Eric felt almost overcome with emotion, with an excitement he could barely contain. This man could not have been a more perfect manifestation of the answers Eric had been looking for.

"In order to have a great time in life, there is one requirement. You have to be calm and cool. You have to be like a hollow bamboo. A hollow bamboo means like a flute, a passageway of unobstructed coolness and lightness."

"How can I be calm and cool; my life is being challenged by so many problems and difficulties. I have so much stress. How can I be calm and cool?"

"If your life is stressed, you have to be *more* calm, *more* cool than the person who is having a great time. If you try to approach a stressful life with greater hyperactivity or with more serious intensity, it's never going to work. You have to let go of all the things that are making you heavy and serious."

"You mean all those things in my life I was complaining about before?"

"What is making you heavy and serious is a set of beliefs. They are coming, not as beliefs, they are coming as thoughts in you. Any thought that tells you that you are not good enough, or tells you that you are going to go down, or tells you this is not a good moment, that you are at the wrong point in your life—it's a superstition."

"Superstition?"

"Superstitions aren't just things like Friday the 13th, those are just nonsense ideas we put into our heads. Someone says, 'Oh my god, she looks so fantastic!' or 'Oh wow, he just won thousands of dollars at the baccarat table!' It *doesn't matter* what you or others are saying. None of it is true. It doesn't matter! You have to remain calm and cool."

"Whether you are going to make a great impact in your own heart or to other people, you have to remain cool enough in your heart. Why do you have to be cool and light? Because that is the nature of the flow of life. The flow of life is very light and cool. It is lighter than even energy and matter, like a clear light. Clear light means to feel a coolness inside you, a light inside you."

"That coolness and lightness inside you, when it goes through you, is almost like inhaling something very cool and clear. If you inhale intelligence, intelligence is actually very light. Intelligence has no heaviness, no boundary, no form, no odor, no color. It's very cool and clear, like a cool breeze. If you inhale it, you are not inhaling through the mouth or the nose, you are inhaling it through every cell. You will feel terrific. All the things you worry about and obsess over—you will see how silly they are, how ridiculous it is to worry about them."

"Inhale intelligence?"

Mark took several deep breaths as the man spoke.

"When I speak about intelligence, I don't mean it as your personal knowledge and smarts. I mean it as the infinite intelligence, that is everywhere in the universe, and which is available to you at any moment, if you are sensitive enough—calm and cool—to connect into it."

"That sounds like God."

"That's a way to say it. All the things you worry about, they are actually about only two things. You are worried about something you heard or said in the past, or else you are worried about something that is going to happen in the future. It is so silly to worry that way. It is so silly to fear and worry about what you heard or said to other people in the past, or the anticipation of something going wrong in the future. Because there is *no* future, there is *no* past. You are here, right now in the present moment, facing infinite intelligence."

"If infinite intelligence is always in front of me, I'm not seeing it."

"Intelligence doesn't appear as a god or a goddess or an angel, or in any kind of form. Intelligence appears right now as whatever you see. You say, 'Oh, no, what I am looking at can't be intelligence. I see chairs and people, that's not intelligence.' No, that *is* intelligence. That is a manifestation of intelligence. Whatever you see in front of you is actually a curtain of intelligence. That curtain is swinging by a cool breeze, in and out, for you to just penetrate through that curtain and get in."

"What does it take to get me through that curtain?"

"It's like you are in an audience looking at a magic show, and the magician is asking for somebody to volunteer to come up to the stage. You want to, but you are afraid, you are nervous and shy. You are scared that somebody will laugh at you or make fun of you. You should have the outrageous heart to say, 'I am the one!' and go onto the stage. Even if others are trying to get to the stage, you can move them aside and *you* go, because you want to feel that way. This is not about competition; this is about your fascination to feel what is on the stage."

"Intelligence is asking you to come out from your stories, all your nonsense ideas, silly thoughts, all the stupid things you worry about – everything. And to create what? It's not to create wealth or get lots of energy. Those are byproducts."

"You are always scheming and planning to get something. Even while you are listening to me you are scheming and planning. You can't help it! You can't stop it, it's a habit. You are listening to me, maybe seventy-five percent, you are listening to yourself with the other twenty-five percent. Emotionally, you are masturbating. It is habitual. You are just scratching at yourself with all kinds of fantasies and future plans."

"What I am talking about is not about creating wealth or energy. That will be easy if you are smart. If you are smart, those things will come to you. Are you smart? You are smart by nature. Not because of your intelligence or your family, but because you are connected to the force of life. That's what makes you smart. Every human being is connected to the forces of life. They have no idea they are connected, so they go about unconsciously. I am trying to wake you up to become conscious and awake and alive."

"If you are awake and alive and conscious, you will not be troubled by your own unworthiness. Without any scheming and planning, you can feel a strength in yourself, an emotional energy. You have to feel like a giant, not in size, but in strength. You have to feel that you can do anything. I'm not talking about physical strength here. I am talking about the strength of knowing you can do anything and you can create anything."

"That kind of confidence—I can't just summon it out of the air."

"Right now, your mind is telling you how you have screwed things up and messed up your life. There is not one human being who did not do stupid things, who did not make mistakes, who did not do things they later felt guilty about. The difference is that some said, 'forget about it!' and they came into the next wave to create and design. Because they were rising up like a great warrior. They knew that mistakes are not who you are. You can drop your self-consciousness and rise above all that."

"Right now, while you are listening to me, your mind is trying to attack you. Anything that is trying to steal your focus and make you feel bad is an attack. I am trying to create a space in you so that you think right. When you can think right, you feel so good. Thinking right is not about thoughts. Thinking right is like singing a song. It doesn't matter if other people are criticizing or critiquing you. When you sing a song, you feel good. Sing a song. It's the same when you think right. When you think right you feel something. What do you feel? You feel the pattern and the rhythm of the things that are moving in front of you."

"Moving in front of me?"

"It doesn't matter what is moving in front of you. It can be the stock market, it can be a game you are playing, or an idea you have, or something you want to produce, it doesn't matter. What matters is that your heart is one hundred percent in it. If your heart is one hundred percent in anything, then you are in a win-win situation. If you feel one hundred percent in your heart, go and do it. If your heart is not in it one hundred percent, just wait till your heart feels one hundred percent right. Don't do anything on impulse. Just wait. This is true for every moment of your life."

"Every moment of your life there is something happening, something is coming to you like a new wave, an opening up of a brilliant idea, a feeling you can create and produce. And if you are not right now tuning into that one hundred percent—just wait. Waiting is actually an incredible pleasure. Waiting is actually another word for *discipline*. What you do not have is discipline. If I ask you to discipline yourself, you will not like it. But if I tell you to wait and then you will see something great, you will love the idea. It doesn't matter what is in your mind, you have to wait. When you can wait, then you will feel something opening. Something will open."

"I want to feel that."

"You should have right thinking for the pleasure of living. Whenever you feel right, it breaks up your unworthiness. Unworthiness comes and says various things to you—you are not qualified, you are not smart, you are not good looking, you are old and weak, this and that, and at the same time it tells you 'be careful.' Never be careful! Be *alert*. Be supremely alert, so alert, so sharp. Have a condensed, razor-sharp focus. Just like a magnifying glass can condense the rays of the sun and burn a hole in your skin, a razor-sharp awareness can burn through any mental walls that are there and open them."

"I understand," said Eric, "the focus is razor-sharp because it's not encumbered by past dogma and interpretation."

"Razor-sharp awareness is like an emotional erection of energy that allows you to break through all the walls. The walls are made out of old thoughts and beliefs. It doesn't matter where they came from—your family, your church, your culture, the news—it doesn't matter. You feel in your heart a fascination, like a huge flame. That flame in your heart has the same energy and force of a great sun that is bursting out with incredible, inconceivable energy. In your heart, the fire is not in the form of a flame, it is contained in the form of a breeze, it is contained in the form of a light. Not the heat light but a clear light. Clear light is what is called a cool light."

"Cool light is like a blue sky. But it is not just a color I am talking about. It's a feeling I am talking about. It's a feeling of such fascination inside you. Inside you there is such a deep fascination for you to rise and become a great man, and to create and produce. Let that fascination brew within you."

"I don't usually allow myself to think about things like that. It seems very indulgent."

"You have to be in love, just like you are in love with a woman. There is a body heat then, and you don't think about it. You feel so great. There is a recognition, and an acknowledgement, and a fire in your heart. That fire will erupt through your heart. It will penetrate through everything and hit the target."

"Somewhere, you feel such a deep love for yourself. It's not a selfishness or a self-love. It's a sense of the deepest love you have, just for being alive in this body, being human. You are so grateful to your parents for creating the passage that allowed you to become alive. That aliveness, being here, allows you to be creative and produce anything you want in your life."

"No matter what has happened in your past up until now, no matter what the other people are saying, all the other things are just superstitions. Your fascination for what you want to do will burn all the thoughts, will burn all those old beliefs away, and you will not even see them, you will not be affected by anything. It's so fascinating, like Nero, you can be playing a violin or guitar even while the world is burning. It doesn't mean you are selfish. Your world is actually a set of beliefs you have built within yourself that keeps this moment from being a moment of spontaneity. It tells you this is not the right moment. It is *always* the right moment for you to create."

"It doesn't matter what you connect with, you can think clearly, and whatever you do will be effortless, will be approached in spontaneity. It won't be tiring for you to create and produce, because you are in love. If making love is a tiring thing, people won't be having sex. People have sex because they never consider making love as an exercise. Exercise is going to the gym. Making love is a connection, so it's a pleasure. It is the pleasure of giving and receiving."

"In the same way, right now is a moment in your life always ready to create an opening. And you can create anything you want to have without all the distractions, doubts and fears that are trying to tell you, 'Wait a minute! This might not be right.' You are not going to argue with any of those thoughts that are there. You are telling yourself 'I love you, and I am coming with you.' You are not telling that to a man or a woman, you are telling that internally to a space of recognition and acknowledgment, that you see something as very right. Fall into that and you will never be hurt, because you are falling in love."

CHAPTER 9

CATCHING THE FLOW

"The nature of the ocean is never-ending waves.
The nature of life is never-ending flow."

An enormous pond, almost a small lake, lay between Mark's hotel and the Las Vegas Strip. A row of trees along the sidewalk further screened the street from their view, as Mark and his companion sat in a café overlooking the water. An array of synchronized fountains at the center of the lake surged in time to 'Nessun Dorma.' Late afternoon light caught the tops of the jets of water. Mark was pensive.

"I have to admit, these times when you're talking, telling me all these things—I'm totally caught up in what you're saying, I'm hanging on every word. But then, after it's over, I can't remember ninety percent of what you said."

"That's because it's coming from a different consciousness. When you're with me, your consciousness is changed, and then, when you are back in your usual patterns, it's hard for you to reconnect to it. That's the same reason many people can't remember jokes. A joke puts you into a different consciousness, as do your dreams."

"I get it. Well, this trip has been different from anything I've ever experienced. It's been like a time-out, like a pause in my life. Aside from you, I've barely talked to anybody since I've been here. I've played a fair amount, but I've spent just as much time watching, walking around, and looking. I look around, and I get this sense that there's so much more going on than I can see, more than I've ever been aware of. I did that thing with the hot water. I took a very hot cup of water, and I just sipped it very slowly. I put my hands together, and I looked in the mirror for a long time."

"I never just sit and do nothing. I'm always going, going, and it never even occurred to me that I could just stay quiet and not do anything. But it's been amazing, to just *not* do things. To *not* do all my usual things, my normal routines. I like action. I remember one thing you said—you said we like friction in our lives, interaction, sex, drama, competition, all that kind of stuff. I feel that. That's how I've always lived, and I never knew any other way. I like action, conquest. I rush into things, and sometimes they blow up. So, it's a huge change for me to just step back and observe. And *appreciate*, just appreciate what's going on around me, without having to rush in and conquer."

The man nodded.

"The nature of the flow is fascinating. It's not something mental or emotional or physical. The flow is reality. The flow just exists. Connecting to the flow is almost like joining a dance. You are watching the dance. It doesn't matter what kind of dance it is. If your mind says, 'This is the wrong kind of dancing,' forget about it. You don't need to know about the dance in order to feel it and have fun and connect to it. It can be a waltz or salsa."

"You are looking at the dance, and there will be one point where you get excited. Don't just walk out onto the dance floor without knowing how to dance. You don't know the motions, how to flow with it. Therefore, you should just wait and see how the other people are dancing and feeling. You can just sit and enjoy the dancing without your mind saying, 'I want to join right now.' Your joining should be natural and spontaneous."

"You are not only having fun; you are connecting into the centrifugal force of the dance floor that is taking people spontaneously into various directions. It is the same way with the stock markets or the casino. Don't think, 'Oh, I know this.' You don't know. You have to remain in a space of fascination, innocence. The mind will try to calculate, 'Oh, I know what is coming.' No. One thing with the intelligence is, it wants to shock you. It is playing with you. You don't realize intelligence has been playing with you, playing with you by giving you the wrong clues. Intelligence likes to toy with you."

"How do I know which are the right clues?"

"You can't catch it with your mind, but you can catch a feeling. You don't catch a realization or a thought or idea, like 'I got it.' Never say 'I got it.' If your heart is exploding with fascination and it is saying 'Yes!' to life, your probability of connecting to the flow is much higher than any other person. You feel right, you feel light."

"Have no judgment. If you have a judgment, don't play at all. If you have a judgment that says, 'Oh, I don't know how to play tennis, but I will try,' don't try! 'Oh, gambling is a bad thing'—don't play then. You have to be excited, almost like a charge when you are about to have sex. It's like a different kind of orgasm. This is an emotional orgasm."

"An emotional orgasm?"

"An emotional orgasm and a physical orgasm, they are parallel realities. In order to have an emotional orgasm, you have to have a warm-up, foreplay, and a feeling of attraction and excitement. You don't go to have sex thinking, 'Oh, after this I can fall into a deep sleep.' In the same way, if you're playing cards, don't think about counting cash. Whatever the game you are playing, the pleasure is not the counting of the cash. The pleasure is the jolt you get from winning, that makes you feel like an innocent boy or girl. Even with a slight win, you should feel yourself emotionally inside, jumping around, cheering."

"You should be like a surfer. A surfer waits. He can sense another wave coming, even if he can't see it. The ocean plays with the surfers. The waves are camouflaged, the ocean goes into a dead calm, and all the people go home. They are cursing, 'I thought there would be good weather for waves today!' The ocean deliberately makes it calm, just to tease you, to see where you are. The surfer doesn't see that suddenly a huge wave is coming. The surfer is not ready to get into it, and so it trashes him. He got trashed because he was distracted."

"That has happened to you many times. Certain bets, playing the stock market, you went with the gut-level hunger, not the fascination or the passion, so you lost it. It's like surfing the wave—you have to catch it just right. The surfer, if the wave comes and trashes him, he laughs, because now he knows. Other people are looking at the horizon, there are no waves at all, so they go home. The surfer waits, because his heart knows another wave is definitely going to come. It has not yet formed at the horizon."

"How does that apply to everyday life?"

"The nature of the ocean is never-ending waves. The nature of life is never-ending flow. The most powerful thing that you need to cultivate is not patience but innocence. Innocence in your heart. If you are trying to be patient, then you are restless, because you are trying to restrain your feelings. You should be in a space of innocence. Then, sooner or later, you will see the new wave coming on the horizon. The horizon recognizes that you are waiting. It waits for a while, then it sends a very smooth wave, that you very gently get into. These are emotions I am talking about. It can be whatever game you are playing with life."

"Innocence is fascination. Fascination makes you cool. People have to cultivate coolness, not patience. That coolness is how you observe in silence the very nature of imperfection. Whatever the game you are playing, you are watching imperfection flowing in front of you. You are watching the play of imperfection. When imperfection sees you watching, you become one with it, and then you can enjoy it. When you know that there is a wave coming, you are not restless. You are at ease. Why? You are waiting to surrender."

Mark nodded his head slowly. The man had said very similar things to him before, but this time he felt the words and their meaning penetrate him completely. He felt an organic understanding of what was said. The man continued.

"So, you go into a huge casino and you are walking around all these machines. Then suddenly there is a $300 million Megabuck. You get close to it and your body goes into heat. Other people didn't even care about that machine, they just saw a couple of donkeys on the screen. But you go near it and you feel it, you have a body heat. And you know now that you will win. And so, you are at ease. If you know that you are the one who will actually connect to it, don't be in any hurry. This is what is called trust. Trust means actually breaking time. If anybody else comes and pulls the handle, you know that's not the right timing. You feel the machine knows your presence and it will wait for you to sit."

"You talk about body heat. Is that passion, excitement?"

"Body heat is the space of attraction. You look at a flower or a beautiful person and you feel something, you sense something. What you sense actually is an opening. Because between two people or two things there is a charged field. But it's not a heat like a temperature. This charge comes out of motion, sound and light. Everything in life has motion, sound and light, visible or invisible, active or inactive. That exists in everything. But the difference is, when you see Niagara Falls, you feel an incredible charged field. Why? Because Niagara Falls has motion, sound and light, and your body has motion, sound and light. Between the two of you, it creates a charged field."

"The charged field allows you to feel one thing – a vanishing point. All the beautiful things, what we see as beauty, are vanishing points. A vanishing point is a point of no-time. All the greatest things in life are about motion, sound and light, that's the fundamental chemistry of the flow of life."

"The motion is not the rotation of the Earth, it's the motion of the universe that's actually going through us. The sound is not a melody, the sound is the space of silence, a reverberation within us. The light is not sunlight. So, when you can see that way for a moment, it will allow you to have no mind, and when you have no mind, you have no memory."

"No mind, no memory means you're not thinking of the past, or based on your past knowledge, right?"

"It means you are not judging things based on your interpretations. If you can look at anything without memory or mind, whatever you see will become beauty. That beauty is actually a point of recognition of absolute innocence in fascination. Without fascination, nothing will work. Without fascination, still you can have sex with someone, but it won't be making love. You are simply masturbating inside each other. That's okay, it's not a big deal, but you're not making love."

"What you are doing in any game of chance, like roulette, or any game of brilliance, like chess, any game that requires you to focus, or use strength and energy, they have one thing in common. There is a zone. That zone, if you can enter, you are leaving all the energy of your story behind. Then, your presence is connected and the force of light will go through you like a lightning bolt. It is that lightning feeling that allows you to see something clearly. It lets you see things through a vanishing point that only you can see and nobody else."

"If you are going to play chess, but your mind says, 'Oh my god, this guy is too tough for me,' don't even play then. One bit of hesitation and you cannot do it. You have to put all your body into it. You are not gambling or playing tennis or hitting a ball – you are making love. In making love to a man or a woman, what you are doing is, you are unleashing yourself. In playing a game or in gambling, you are unleashing your presence. You are unleashing your presence, not your ideas, not your thoughts. When you unleash your presence, what will be around you will be motion, sound and light."

"When you say 'unleash your presence,' does it mean to just be who you really are?"

"Yes."

"And you say the motion, sound and light will be around you—does that mean to see something beyond . . . what does that mean?"

"It's not something you see. You feel the oneness of the focus. When the focus becomes one, it is no longer focus at all. Then it becomes complete clarity, and that's very powerful. That means you don't discriminate or judge — you see everything around you."

Mark said, "You see everything without judging. All right. I'm trying to get this."

"This is something you can cultivate. It's not like you just hear this and say, 'Oh, okay, I got it now.' You have to cultivate a space within you in order to become a player. You are not just playing games, you are playing with life. This is an invitation to play with life."

"You know," said Mark, "I always felt a little guilty, because the fact is, I love to play with life, and certain people I know have maybe thought I was not a serious person, or not very mature. But you make it sound like it's my patriotic duty to play with life. I'm being a little jokey here, but sincerely, I appreciate that."

The man reached over and squeezed Mark's shoulder, then wagged a finger at him.

"Life presents all these games because life knows you are not alert. It is asking you to be alert, ready and willing. All the games and man-made ideas, we build this whole thing. Life has no interest in punishing or destroying you. It wants to play with you. It's almost like life is saying, 'What the hell! All these years, why couldn't you play with me?' Life wants to play with you, understand this. Life doesn't care about your relationships; it doesn't care about anything you claim to be or the problems you have. The invitation of life is to make the impossible possible."

"That's my password. But why do we not get the invitation to play with life?"

"You are not focused. You are in greed. Not just you—everybody. So, all kinds of things are set up in the world, stock markets, all kinds of financial games, casinos. What do the casinos say? 'You are claiming you are psychic? You are claiming you can predict? You are claiming you can see? Okay, baby! Come and get it!' And people go into it like a mouse trap."

"You are attracted to the mouse trap because you are greedy. And that greediness actually allows you to experience one thing—fear. You are playing games with fear. If you want to make love, you don't make love with fear. If you are horny and you see a stranger and you want to make love, but then you feel like, 'Oh, I don't know, she might be up to no good,' don't do it. You are going to regret it."

"Amen, brother."

"In that same way, if you feel like, 'Oh, I don't have money, I have to get some money. Maybe I can gamble and by some fluke I will win some money,' don't do it! You will fail. You have to have a burning fascination to see the flow, to observe. You have to be at ease to watch it, any game. Just like the way you watch a sunrise or a sunset, in fascination. You cannot have one single word or thought going in your mind in that moment of fascination."

"Remember, playing is not guessing. All throughout, you are guessing, that's why you fail. It doesn't matter what the game is. You are guessing. When your body is actually feverish with desire and greed, you are not going to enjoy anything. In any game, you are not playing against life, you are playing *with* life. You are never playing against life. You cannot play against life. People who lose at a game may think, 'Life is against me.' No, life is never against you. People blame the world; they blame life when they lose."

"I'm trying to figure you out," Said Mark, "because the way you talk, you sound spiritual, but you're really not, are you?"

"I am not teaching you meditation or religion or other things. This is not a teaching. This is just plain common sense. Any child could understand what I am saying. You don't have to be clever. Play is a part of the nature of life. Any game is play and it is part of nature and part of innocence."

"Life is play. Understand, there is nothing good or bad, wrong or right, about play. Play is an invitation. You have to see it that way. I don't have any judgment about the game you are playing, I am only showing you the very simple nature of reality, which is actually held as a big secret by stock markets and the casinos. 'No, you can't do this. You can't beat the house. You are too stupid.' That's what they are telling you."

"But it's not so!" said Mark.

Then, "So, do you have any more gambling tips you'd like to share?"

"If you want to play any game, go happily. Otherwise, don't play. If you want to swim, you need to wear a bathing suit. If you want to run, you need to have running gear. In the same way, if you are going to play chess, or play at the casino—dress very nicely. Don't dress like an idiot. Dress up in order for you to feel good with yourself. When you see yourself in the mirror, you see you are dressed nicely. You are not overdressed, you are not dressing to impress, you are dressed so that you feel good. And before you begin to play, go and pee. Why? Because you have to empty your body. Don't play with any heaviness in your body."

"Copy that."

"And when you are coming out of the restroom, don't be in a rush to come out. Look at yourself in the mirror. Put your left hand over your heart and your right palm to the mirror and touch it and tap it. Have a smile with yourself and tell yourself something sweet. Don't say, 'I am going to win.' Say, 'I love you.' Say something very profound and real and truthful to you. Then tell yourself, 'I am going to feel the flow. I want to feel the flow. I want to see how it comes. I want to catch the imperfection. I want to feel it.'"

"Why is the mirror so important?"

"Whenever you look in the mirror and you touch the mirror, you are acknowledging motion, sound, and light. You are not connecting to your story. You are acknowledging the presence of motion, sound, and light in you and around you."

"The great Olympic swimmers, when they are in the water, they don't feel their body, because they become one with the flow of the water. The Olympic runners don't have a sense about their running, they are not thinking they're running, they become that motion itself. They feel like something is being unleashed out of themselves."

"How does that relate to me?"

"You have to stop the one game you have been playing all your life—trial and error. You guessed. You went with what you thought was right. That's not sensing, those are all mind traps. Desire can lure you into the mousetrap. But here you are not going to smell whether it is cheese or not because you are not a mouse. You are able to sense the trap. You are sensing life."

"Those who discovered the greatest principles and the laws of nature, and those who made the greatest discoveries of the universe, they are all people who sensed the space and activated the right signal and created equations. Newton, Einstein, Galileo."

"The vibration comes into mathematics. Math is actually a game. If math was introduced to children like a casino game, everybody would be brilliant. It would entice people to see the flow. Math is all flow. We are using numbers to indicate the patterns and designs that are happening in the world. Because the patterns and designs are not just four directions, they are infinite."

"If you are able to somehow or other feel and get into this incredible flow, you can never come out disappointed. Because you don't actually have a goal to achieve. You are not doing this for the specific goal of winning millions. You are playing this game for the fun of it."

"That's an advantage I have," said Mark, "I don't need the money. I never come here desperate to get rich. I put down enough money that I feel it, feel the stakes, but not enough to make or break me."

"Most people go to the casinos half-anxious. If you are half-anxious, don't make love! All the things I am telling you are illuminations for you to feel. They are the appetizers, emotional sorbets I am giving. When you hear these things, you will feel excited to go and play, because you see the other side of the game. I am revealing to you the other side of the game. That will allow you to see that life itself is fun. Everything you are doing right now is serious, and you can change that."

"Interesting you say that: everything I do is serious. It's true, even though I'm outwardly pretty upbeat. But I have a lot of doubt, a lot of guilt. Not many people see that."

"I am just bringing to the surface the magical child within you. Whatever looks impossible appears magical because we can't see how it happens. Magic is a trick of time-space. You are a magical child, and I am revealing what the magician has done. So, you are going to catch the flow and get your life flourishing, because that will allow you to have no doubt. This is bringing you into a state of no doubt. When you have no doubt, you don't have to think about love, it naturally comes to you. This is a win-win, fun situation."

"It's hard for me to have fun. Why is it so hard to just have fun?"

"All humans have one thing: unworthiness. Unworthiness is not a darkness. The opposite of unworthiness is not worthiness. Unworthiness actually has no opposite. It only looks like it should have an opposite, like worthiness or brilliance. No. Nighttime is not the bad side of life. Daytime is not the good side of life. They are part of the natural flow. Unworthiness doesn't say you are bad or weak or inferior."

"How the unworthiness comes to your life is very simple. You want to have an absolutely wonderful life, to have money and ideas flowing to you, and unworthiness says, 'It's too good to be true.' Unworthiness doesn't come and say you are weak. It says, 'Whatever you think you want—it's too good to be true *in your case*. In your case, not other people, just you.' It tells you that you have been a humbug, that you have manipulated, done this or that."

"What it is telling you is part of human nature. It is there in everyone. There is no perfect human being who exists; unworthiness is always there. In order to get out of the unworthiness, there are a few things I am just putting into you, and if you would like, you can write them down and look at them later.

The first thing is:

Nothing is too good to be true.

Second thing is:

This moment has nothing to do with any other moment in your life.

And the third one is:

Let it come. Let it rise.

"Those are like passwords. They open your heart into a realization of humbleness."

"The opposite of trust is not doubt. Trust is actually love. Love is something that comes to you. Love is your nature. Trust is also your nature. We are built on love and trust. Otherwise, we could never have built this incredible world. But they are very subtle. They stay in a state of non-interference. That non-interference is actually the wave of the motion, sound, and light that we have in our body. It's in our body. If you tune into that, you will not hear the sound of your echo, your inner dialogues. You will experience a very powerful sensuousness."

"The nature of the play in any game is lost when you are bored with yourself. So, you are trying to play almost like to stimulate yourself. It doesn't work that way. Play should be a state of attraction. Play is attraction, whatever the game you are playing."

"All the playful things are not actually games, they are the opening and constructing of various patterns of thinking, through which you realize or recognize the nature of the flow. The nature of the flow is stunning and shocking. It's not like you see the nature of the flow and then you say, 'Oh, I got it, now I understand.' No, it's not an understanding."

"The flow is going through your body from the time you are born until you are no longer living. Part of the game of life is that life never shows you the entrance point of your birth, or the exit point when your life is over. It just tells you, 'Happy Birthday!' Whenever you celebrate your birthday, it's not like you are born again, it's about celebrating and appreciating your birth, your entrance. Part of the game is that you don't know the beginning or the end—it's very strange. All the other games we know of, like chess or basketball, we know where they begin and end. But not the game of life. The game of life doesn't allow you to know. No one remembers their birth. That is called non-interference."

"The first sacred law of the game of life is non-interference. You don't interfere. You have to just see things the way they are, without interfering. And when you can see things as they are without interfering, that becomes an excitement. Because you are seeing something. What are you seeing? It is a pattern of motion, sound, and light that exists inside you and around you. To see motion, sound, and light inside and around you is a tremendous jump-start to your heart. Because at birth you could not get it. You were unconscious. You just became conscious—that was the waking-up process."

"And also, when you are leaving, life doesn't want you to leave with any baggage, so when you are leaving, you don't know that you have left. So, your birth and death are a form of grace."

The fountains began to surge in time to a new song, as lights beneath the water shone upwards into the twilight air, to the tune of 'One Singular Sensation.' Mark and the man sat in silence until the song was over.

"Okay, buddy, I'll see you," said the man, high-fived Mark, and departed.

Mark sat a while longer, staring in wonder at the water below.

CHAPTER 10

HEART TRUST

"See something that is funny.
See something that is joyful.
See something that is beautiful."

The ballroom was nearly empty. The panelists and audience had filed out, and Eric was on the phone with the hotel's liaison, requesting that housekeeping come to reset the room. Audio-visual technicians rolled their equipment carts across the carpeted floor. Eric had not been a participant in the discussion, but had watched from the side of the hall, making sure there were no technical problems. Everything had gone smoothly. Another day of the conference had come to a successful conclusion. Eric gathered up the stray pens and folders left on the panelists' tables, walked down the steps from the stage, and headed for the rear exit doors.

A lone figure was sitting in the last row. Eric recognized him as he drew closer. The man stood up and greeted him.

"Congratulations," he said as he shook Eric's hand and clapped him on the back, "I think that went very well, don't you?"

"Thanks, yes, it went well," said Eric.

"And when is your presentation?"

"Tomorrow morning."

"It's the keynote speech, isn't it?"

"That's right," said Eric.

"That's fantastic. It's going to get a lot of attention."

Eric swallowed, "Yes."

"Are you ready?"

"Well, I may feel differently about this tomorrow, but right now I feel rather calm. I've written it all down, exactly what I want to say, and I'm going to stand at the podium and read what I've written. I know I can do that. And if they don't like it, what's the worst that can happen?"

The man nodded. Eric took a deep breath.

"I have to say this. I could never have found the words, or the courage, without your influence and guidance. You brought it out of me, and I'm profoundly grateful to you."

The man bowed his head.

Eric said, "Some of the greatest contributions in science, in human knowledge, came in the form of dreams, visions or poems. And the greatest minds were able to take those visions and find their expression in natural phenomena, like the way James Watson saw the double helix structure of DNA in a dream. He dreamed of two snakes intertwined, and he made the connection to the problem he was working on. Maybe my vision as a kid, of all the hearts beating, is pointing to something, something about electrical connections over distance, or energetic fields around our physical bodies, I don't know what, but I think it's an example of what you called infinite intelligence—something that's in the air, that we can all connect to."

"That's beautiful," said the man, "you are onto something, and your passion to know can lead you to discover what it is."

"Do *you* know what it is?" asked Eric, then laughed.

The man smiled.

"No one can give you the answers, it's only by your passion to explore and find out that you develop the faculties to be able to understand and express what it is you are seeking. Do you understand? You are not just looking for answers, you have to expand your awareness in order to accommodate the knowledge you are seeking."

Eric slowly restated the words: "You have to expand your awareness to accommodate the knowledge you are seeking. I see what you're saying. One problem is, I have so many distractions. I have all these practical concerns of the money, all the stuff I go through with my kids, the challenges of my practice, the patients, my marriage—these are all things I really care about, but I'm also trying to clear my vision so that I can pursue something that is very tenuous, very subtle."

The man shifted in his chair and cleared his throat.

"There are three things people worry about, whether consciously or unconsciously. Number one is their health. One way or another, there is an anxiety about health or your body. Number two is money. It doesn't matter whether you have a thousand dollars or a billion, you don't think you have enough, or it won't come the way you want to have it. Number three is very interesting, it is relationships. Most people's relationships are very fragile, and as a result they are always looking for somebody or something. What happens with these three things is, they are making you feverish. That feverishness is very bad for you. It makes it so you can't enjoy the search, whatever you are searching for. There is nothing wrong with searching for money, good health or relationships, but most people do it feverishly, and as a result they lack the fascination, they lack the trust, they lack the connection to their heart. So, they never truly get what they are seeking."

"Now, your particular case is a little different. You have a great life. Your situation financially is pretty good, right?"

"More or less."

"Your health is good, and your relationships are good. Only problem is, you have a lot of maintenance to do to keep everything going, and so you feel tired. You feel you don't have the energy or the time to do what you really want. That's what is making you feel desperate and feverish."

"All of these searches that people are engaged with—it's like being an addict. They have an emotional addiction to these searches, because the searches confirm one thing about them. It confirms the unworthiness in them. You see them in the casino. Even if they win money, they lose. It's called 'the gambler's law.' You win, and then you lose. You don't start off losing, you win first. You win at first because of innocence. They call it 'beginner's luck,' but it's not luck. You win at first, because you are in a state of fascination. You don't know anything about how it works, so the fascination connects you to the flow of probability and possibility. You feel something, and you act on it. Then you feel good, it feeds your mind, then you think you know it, you think you've got it."

"The moment you think you know something, it's very interesting, it brings the ego into it. You think, 'I've got a woman,' 'I've got money,' 'I'm in great shape.' You can't think that way. You have to be at ease with everything, cool with everything. If you are cool, then it's a mindfulness, an awareness, an observation. And that's what I want you to have."

"I've got a ways to go before I'm cool with everything."

"This is something very important to understand about your life, and what you are trying to manifest and create in order to have a great life. You have a sense of your own unworthiness. Unworthiness is not something that goes away, and it's not a negative part of your being."

"It's not negative?"

"It's like a shadow. A shadow only occurs when there is sunlight. You don't see a shadow when you are in darkness. If you are already feeling bad, you're bad. But when you are feeling good, when you are alert, when you feel like life is good and life is flowing and things are happening, somehow or other you will do something to take you down. It's called sabotage. This sabotage is not an accident. It is not a distraction or a distortion. Sabotage is one of the ways you are convincing yourself of the very fragile nature of life. Impermanence means, very simply, you can't hold anything. When you can't hold anything, it makes you feel very insecure and unsteady. You can't hold your woman, your job, your health, anything."

"But impermanence is not a bad thing, right?"

"Truly speaking, impermanence is not your enemy. Unworthiness does one thing to you: it interrupts one of the greatest strengths of your being. It interrupts one of the greatest centers of your innocence: trust. Trust is not a belief, and it's not a knowing. It's not something you experience by getting something or releasing something else."

"The innocent newborn baby experiences trust, and that trust is what enables them to recognize their matrix, that is, their mom and dad, who provide them with energy, security and possibility, and to feel good about their arrival. But for the baby it is unconscious and involuntary. For the baby, establishing trust with their matrix is unconscious. For you, right now, no matter how old you are, you need to establish trust with your matrix. You have a matrix, given by no one, forming from your own fascination, heart drive and heart awakening."

"There is a matrix you are creating and designing as you go, from your own innocence and from your own fascination, that allows you to be at ease in the world, in the space you are creating. When you are at ease in the space you are creating, you experience freedom not as a release, but as living intelligence."

"For your whole life, in many ways, whatever you experienced was given to you. Or, better said, you were dependent on other people, dependent on your parents, dependent on the knowledge you have. Your life was dependent on so many things for so long. And because of your dependent nature, you never got the flavor of what trust is. So, as a result, trust became belief to you, knowledge, a way you tried to create order, and manipulated in various ways. Trust is none of those things. Trust is pure love, the pure essence of your presence. Whenever that trust is interrupted in any way, you go off-balance."

"Being off-balance is like having a dislocated shoulder. You can live that way, of course, but you don't want to live with a dislocated shoulder. In this case, it's a dislocation of emotional balance, your emotional alignment. Emotional alignment is not a knowing, and it's not an energy. It is, however old you are, innocence. Innocence is the uninterrupted sweetness about you that is always there."

"That's very beautiful," said Eric, "It seems like, rather than innocence, we feel that we need to acquire all kinds of power and mastery. But innocence is not incompatible with strength, is it?"

"The sweetness and innocence of our presence—when we don't feel it, we do the worst things. What do we do? We drink, we take drugs, we do bizarre, weird things, all of which are artificial ways of kicking us into experiencing some kind of power, but power is not actually what you get."

"Power is, in a sense, feeling you can go out of control. What you are trying to do is to go out of control. It doesn't have to be drugs or alcohol, you may have some bizarre emotional eruptions, crazy weird things you like to do. Extreme ones are like the crazy people who take guns and go shoot people or shout at them. You don't have such weird expressions. If you are ever shouting at anybody you love, it means you are off-balance with trust. And if you are shouting at somebody you can't stand, then it's even worse. It's almost like the law of reverse effort."

"So, all these weird expressions come out of a feeling of powerlessness? How do I get out of it?"

"I am sending you blue waves of various emotional, not intelligence—innocence—that can wash away the attempts of your unworthiness to make you accident-prone, to make you vulnerable and fragile. It's not a conscious attempt, what your unworthiness does, it's an emotional reflex, where somehow or other you are telling yourself, 'It's too good to be true,' for you to have the greatest life. With or without your knowledge, you are telling yourself, 'I can have an okay, balanced life, but it is definitely too good to be true for me to have brilliant health, happiness and endless joy with my life.' So, you are committing little emotional sabotages that affect, not your knowledge, but your trust. Trust is your presence."

"You said, 'Trust is your presence.' Let me see if I understand that. Trust is feeling that you have no need to protect or defend or pretend."

"Yes."

"And when you have no need to protect or defend, you feel free to be exactly who you are."

"Yes."

"And being exactly who you are is your presence."

"Yes. I am trying to get you to experience this great wave that I am opening up for you, so you can get carried away. It's a wave you can surf. Those who are not alert, they run away from the wave, but you are a lover of life, a great sorcerer, an adventurer, so this is a wave, if you get into it, that will take you and wash away the unworthiness. Unworthiness is never totally eliminated, because it is not a negative or a positive thing.

It is part of our life process, almost like an excretion, like a bowel movement or urination. They are not bad, they are good. They empty the unnecessary stuff. The unworthiness is a way you can flush out what is unwanted in your emotions."

"That's fascinating. You're saying it's not a neurosis, it's a natural process."

"It is very important that you see this moment of your life and not try to defend or feel safe or create some kind of order. Don't justify, rationalize and compensate. You don't need to do that. Try not to do that. And if you feel your mind is telling you to do these things, you can make a note, write it in your notebook and keep track of it. This is a time for you to feel an incredible rain of innocence, a rain of brilliance that will come to wash your heart so it can open and blossom. You are here in life to blossom, to open totally, absolutely. Only when you are trying to open totally do little distractions come and say, 'What do you think you're trying to do?'"

"Trust is the most powerful feeling. When the trust blossoms, it is no longer trust, it is awakening. In awakening, you are very conscious, you see very clearly. You see with such clarity, because you see with complete fascination."

"Why don't we have trust?" asked Eric, "Is it because of negative experiences we've had? Can I just dismiss all doubt from my mind? How do I do that?"

"Trust is never based upon a dogma or a conviction. You trust in God or angels or the dollar bill or whatever, because you don't trust yourself. There is only one person you have to trust: the person who appears in your mirror every day. Every morning somebody appears in your mirror—you should smile at that person, not frown. Just smile. If you don't smile at yourself, you are not in trust, meaning you doubt the person in the mirror. Establishing trust is establishing love with yourself. Establishing love with yourself is very important for you to feel that you are good and you are right."

"Do you have any suggestions for how I can do this?"

"I would like you to discover three things. The first thing I want you to discover is, what is fascination? Second thing is, what does it mean to be alert? And the third thing I want you to discover is, what is surrender, or another way to say it is, can you have no resistance? With or without your knowledge, you have some resistance that is running in your body, making you serious. Discover why you are resisting. See something that is funny, see something that is joyful, see something that is beautiful. It will unlock your resistance."

"Let me write this down," said Eric as he reached for a pen, "What is fascination? What does it mean to be alert? And the third was?"

"What is surrender—what does it mean to have no resistance?"

"Got it. And then, see something funny, see something joyful, and?"

"See something that is beautiful."

"Got it."

"Good. Now, shall we go?"

They walked out of the conference hall and into the grand hallway that led back to the hotel and the casino. Large mirrors hung on the walls on either side of them, and as they walked past, Eric saw their reflections multiplied in the opposing mirrors, curving back into infinity.

The man smiled.

"Tomorrow is your big day. You are in a good space. Just look in the mirror whenever you think of it. Look in the mirror, touch your heart and tap the mirror, and then tell yourself something very good about you. Unfortunately, I can't be there for your presentation, but actually that will be better for you. Why don't we meet in the evening for drinks? There is a bar at the top of the hotel, let's say at seven o'clock."

"All right, that will be great. I'm sorry you won't be there for the talk, but thank you, thank you so much for everything."

"Oh yes, of course. All right, I'll see you tomorrow. Bye."

He veered off abruptly in the direction of the casino and Eric continued back to his room. Now that he was alone, he reflected on the dreamlike quality of his interactions with the man.

"Here I am," Eric thought to himself, "in Las Vegas, about to do something completely out of character, egged on by a complete stranger with no name. Who is he? And more to the point, who am I?"

Chapter 11

The Ocean of Fascination

"What you have today, what you see today, you have not seen before."

Mark was sitting in the hotel's VIP lounge, sunk deep in an overstuffed chair. A cup of coffee and a chocolate chip cookie sat on the side table next to him. Urns of coffee and hot water, pastries, bagels, and an array of teas were on a sideboard under the attentive care of a uniformed attendant. Behind the concierge counter, smartly dressed employees catered to their elite guests in hushed tones. One end of the lounge led to the atrium. At the other end were doors to private offices. To the right of these, glass double doors led to a bank of elevators and a corridor back to the casino. Now and then, someone would go in or out through the door into the atrium, and the sounds of the casino would intrude.

Mark was excited, but also agitated. In the morning, he would be flying back to New York. He felt he was on a new road, and he was eager for more guidance. The man had come into his life like a bolt of lightning, and soon he would be gone. He had deflected all Mark's attempts to pin down his identity and origin, and Mark had not pressed him any further. But now he felt he had to do something. He resolved that he would not let the man get away without telling him his name, and how he knew what he knew.

The man entered from the atrium, exchanged greetings, and sat down opposite Mark.

"How are you doing?" he asked. Mark answered without hesitation.

"I always thought I had a great life. Or I should say, I *assumed* I had a great life, because I had all the things people want. I make a lot of money.

I'm a fairly young, good-looking Wall Street guy. There are magazines that are telling me how great I am, all the amazing stuff I can buy. And it *is* great. But I'm seeing how it could even be way, way greater. I want my life to have a certain amount of excitement, but I'd like to do something where I'm not just trying to pile up more money. For instance, I'm amazed at what I've learned from you, I don't even have words for it, and I'd like to help you reach the whole world with whatever it is you do. You could write a book, just based on the things you've told me, and I know it would be a best seller. I would completely finance it for you. It would be a huge success. What do you think about that?"

The man laughed.

"I think something like that could be great for you. But tell me, are you enjoying your trip? You seem a little tense."

"I don't know if *enjoy* is the right word, but this has been an amazing trip! I'm seeing things in a different way. I'm thinking about my wife a lot. I miss her. Besides you, she's the one person who really showed me I could be a different person. I wish she could meet you. We never came to Vegas together. I used to come here before we were married, and this is the first time since then. I didn't think it was her type of thing. But what I've felt this week, I really want to share *that* with her."

The man said, "For her to love you, and to marry you, there is something in you that she sees, something you yourself don't see yet. Think about that. You don't really know who you are. You've only seen a little slice of who you are."

"Yes," said Mark, "I can feel that. Listen, by the way, I'm leaving tomorrow morning, and I would very much like to see you again. I joked about paying you, but seriously, I *would* pay you for more . . . instruction. Let me give you my card. Please, call me if you're in New York."

"Oh, thank you," said the man. He took the card without looking at it.

"Do you have a card, or anything? Could I get your email?" said Mark.

"Oh yes, we can do that later, definitely. You know, I like what you said about your wife. She provokes new things in you, new emotions. That's very important."

"I've felt a lot of new emotions this week. I'm not even sure what to call some of the things I've felt."

"Some of them don't have names. You are exploring new territory within you, just like exploring the Earth. The Earth is surrounded by a great ocean. And we are also surrounded by a great ocean. Our ocean is actually an ocean of emotions. We have the seven seas, and inside us are the seven tears."

"When you are swimming in the ocean, what is it you feel? Openness. We have a sense of vastness when we are feeling at ease emotionally. If you can be at ease, just focusing on your presence, you can feel that vastness. If you can do that, then you are in a very powerful space, looking at the right thing."

"How we see our emotions is very important. Do your emotions intrigue you or captivate you? Normally, it's not your emotions you are in touch with, it is your thinking. Actually, you are not really truly thinking, you are having thoughts. All the thoughts are just *stuff.* All that stuff is just emotional clutter, like junk in your closet. You try to keep your house in order so that you will feel good."

"I like that distinction: we aren't thinking, we're having thoughts. You're saying we don't usually control our thoughts; we're not consciously deciding what we want to think about."

"That's right."

"And the same is true for our emotions? We can choose what we want to *feel,* too? That's something I never even considered. I thought emotions just *happened.*"

"You don't realize it, but you are able to create a little emotional pattern or design that makes you feel good. It's very powerful if you can do that, because it allows you to experience one thing: focus. Without the correct focus, you can't really see or feel clearly your own innocence."

"Your innocence is the childlike nature you have within you. You feel that innocence within yourself as the truth about you. If you are manipulating yourself or others, it's not that you are a bad person, but you won't be feeling clean or clear. Innocence means virgin, untainted, pristine. It allows your emotions to run very cleanly. If you have unconditional, uncontaminated feelings, then you feel good. You feel good for no reason, not because you have money or a great job. You just feel good about *you*."

"It's not about the world, it's about you. It allows you to be captivated by your own presence. If you are captivated by your own presence, then when you look into the mirror and see yourself, you will see your image as if it is a great painting coming at you. That's a very pleasant shock to your system."

"The pleasure of life actually comes to you through the innocence. It is a space within you. You may think of yourself as rough and tough, but by nature you are innocent and pure. There is something within you that is so true and clean and clear. It has nothing to do with who you are, or your past and what you have done. It is the nature of the space that is within you. Whatever you do in life, whether you are an architect, an engineer, an artist, whatever you do, that becomes an expression of your innocence."

"I never thought of myself as innocent," said Mark, "even when I was a kid. But I think I understand what you mean by innocent. It's feeling like everything is happening for the first time, everything is new."

"Yes, but we have become so conditioned emotionally throughout our life that our pleasure has become really a form of masturbation, whether physically, mentally, or emotionally. What that means, in essence, is you keep wanting to go back and touch one thing – your story. You keep looking back and touching your story, which is your past. That actually makes you too worn out to make love. And also, it makes you feel *guilty*. Life is telling you that you are here to celebrate life. Life has invited you to a celebration. You are here, not to masturbate, but to make love. Sex is just a small part of that making love. Making love means connecting, merging, and unleashing yourself."

"When you can unleash yourself, then you disappear. You don't have any story then. Then you can have fun with life. Having fun is not just playing with yourself. You have to experience making love. Making love is actually an incredible creation. Having sex and creating a baby is a very unique type of creation. But you can also materialize an incredible creation that comes out of your heart."

"Making love means connecting and opening into something new, right now. If it is not a new feeling or experience you are creating today, then, without your knowledge, you are still just masturbating emotionally and mentally about yesterday. The effect of that is to make you serious, not playful."

Mark narrowed his eyes playfully.

"You sure talk about masturbation a lot! It's okay, I don't judge. No, I'm kidding. You're talking about rehashing the past, being nostalgic and sentimental, right? Like looking through your old photo albums and feeling pathetic."

"That's right. Thinking about your past makes you serious and heavy. Your life should not be like a novel you keep reading and re-reading. Your life should be like a novel you are *writing*. And you are writing it without knowing what the next chapter contains. You are in suspense and excitement, that's what you are here for."

"But right now, you are telling yourself that you know where you are going. If you know where you are going already, then it's not fun. Your novel, called 'The Story of My Life' contains a certain kind of flow, but like any story, it is exciting only because it is a series of surprises. It has suspense coming through various surprises."

"Yes," said Mark, "like you, for instance. If I were writing the story of my life, this chapter right now would be pretty hard to believe."

"What you have today, what you see today, *you have not seen before.* There is a new provocation coming, wherever you are. Whenever somebody asks you how you are doing, you should answer them, 'I am being provoked! I am being challenged!' If you say, 'Oh, I am fine,' that's very boring. You should be excited to interact with life with an incredible fire and fascination. There is a whole new set of challenges and provocations awaiting you each day. They are coming, and you are trying to somehow find a way to make peace and harmony with them. You think, 'I'm not in the mood for challenges. I don't feel daring. I don't want to be outrageous. I need a break, I'm tired.'"

"It is because you feel tired and without energy that you need a push. There is an energy you have available to you that you are not tapping into. There is the normal energy that you use to get by and to create a certain order in your life. That order is what is actually making you go to sleep. If you want to have a powerful life, you need to capture something very powerful and arousing that you have never seen before. Always, there is an invitation that is coming out of infinite intelligence, trying to engage you, attract you, get your attention, but you are distracted by all these other things. Life is asking you to pay attention, to be alert and aware. Life wants you to be mindful, then you will see some new emotional patterns rising on your own horizon."

"That sounds great, but how do I really learn to see that? What do you mean by emotional patterns?"

"Let's start very simply. How awake, alert, and observant are you today? You are awake to your five senses, but how awake are you to your feelings and emotions? Within you is a great ocean. How aware are you of that ocean of emotion? Unless you are directing your emotions and feelings to a specific point, then, with or without your knowledge, you are getting serious. When you get serious, there are two things you ask yourself: 'How are you?' and 'What are you doing?' And what is your answer? *Same old, same old.*"

"It's not actually a conversation you are having with yourself. Having a conversation with yourself is a very different thing. Very rarely does that ever happen. If you were to truly have a conversation with yourself, it is almost like you are really meeting intelligence. It presents you with a powerful spectrum of energies."

"Is that like what you were saying about thinking and thoughts? You said we usually just have random thoughts, not directed thinking."

"You can direct your thinking, and you can direct your emotions, too. Normally, instead of having conversations with yourself, what you are doing is, you are *warning* yourself. What you are saying to yourself is a warning. You are warning yourself, because there is a history, a pattern you have, that says you are going to screw up. You carry guilt about all the mistakes you made. You don't call your mistakes part of the imperfection and impermanence. You take them very personally. You tell yourself, 'It's not because of the imperfection, it's because I'm stupid.'"

"Life says one thing to you: If you want to have a good time, you have to be daring. You have to be lion-hearted, fearless. You have to do something that you will truly be fascinated about. You invite intelligence to come and fill that gap, so that you can exercise your imagination, and your emotional capacity, in order to create and experience something new. It doesn't matter what it is."

"I think I'm pretty daring, actually," said Mark, "I'm not fearful, generally. But I've never had a strong direction in my life, something to be fearless *about*. I haven't had anything bigger than myself, bigger than sex, money and power, as you said."

"You can't just say 'I am adventurous and daring,' you have to provoke the right challenge to come to you. You have to prompt the right query, then the right invitation will come to you. Right now, the things you have invited into your life, they were not summoned by intelligence. They were summoned by your gut-level desire, which is unworthiness."

"Unworthiness can trick you and make you feel something is very good for you, whether it is an idea or a person. What you need is for the right provocation to come, then you can create the correct equation. You have to create an emotional equation that will open a new space for you. You have to be soaked with emotional intelligence. You have to sprinkle yourself with innocence. Innocence is spotless simplicity—uncorrupted, uncontaminated fascination for life. That's how you get intrigued and captivated by where you are right now, today. That will attract you to the right thinking and the right feeling."

"Your innocence has never changed from your birth to today. You have a magical child inside of you. Outside, you look like a gangster, but whatever you have that you are carrying, it's camouflage. For you to truly feel the emotional energy of bravery and daring and fearlessness—they are incredible fires—you have to feel that now. You have to feel a fearlessness *now* in your own true presence. You say, 'Oh, I was courageous.' No. What you felt earlier was attraction, lust. Those are the ones that ran your life."

"You need a different way now. You have to be awake and watchful, you have to pay attention, open your eyes and become sensitive and alive. Then you are not feverish, you are calm and cool. It's a very powerful space. You are worked up in a very nice way, not by mental and emotional masturbations and fantasies. You are worked up because you are seeing the *truth*."

"Your life may be very good right now, but it can me much juicier. In order to have a juicy life, you need one thing, called *spontaneity*. Right now, you are not spontaneous. Because you are not spontaneous, you lack the emotional reflexes that would allow you to *recognize*, *acknowledge*, and *appreciate* what you see. If you do not recognize, acknowledge, and appreciate what you see, then you are not truly having fun, because then it's all very mechanical and superficial. You're not truly feeling it. You have to *feel* it. That feeling is what makes you very alive, awake and sensitive."

"You are not spontaneous right now because you are afraid, you are nervous. That nervousness is keeping you from being spontaneous. When you are spontaneous you are sending signs and signals. Right now, no signs or signals are coming out of you. There is actually a shower of emotions that is wanting to get out of your body. Those emotions want to overflow. They want to reveal and disclose to you feelings and ideas that can be so outrageous."

"You know when you have a massage," said Mark, "and you go into it thinking you're feeling fine—no major aches and pains? And then, when they start working on you, you realize you have all this pain in your muscles, all kinds of unconscious tightness and pain that you were totally unaware of. Well, I feel like that with my emotions. There's so much going on that I wasn't aware of."

"You are good, but you are trying to create peace and harmony. That's great for when you are going to sleep. But when you are awake and alive, you have to experience—not *peace*—freedom and choice, non-interference, unconditional love, silent, sweet surrender. Those are the new brilliant flavors you have yet to taste. They are incredible emotional flavors of intelligence. How do you taste non-interference? Right now, you have all these crazy thoughts going, constant inner dialogues, consciously and unconsciously happening within you. They are distracting you and keeping you from giving your whole presence to this moment. The thoughts are like little dust particles just floating around, buzzing around you, creating within you all kinds of emotional trash. And you are holding onto that. All these thoughts and emotions you are collecting, they are just rubbish. Rubbish is heavy. All the things you scream and shout at yourself, that's all rubbish. Whenever you yell at yourself, that settles down in your system as rubbish, making you heavy."

"How do I get rid of all the rubbish? And how do I stop collecting it?"

"What non-interference means is, you don't engage with your inner dialogues, or with your story. That's very powerful. Normally, you are engaging with your inner dialogues, like a politician, negotiating. 'I can do this,' 'I will do that.' If you know you will be doing those things, then why do you have to tell yourself that? Because somewhere, you have *doubt*. You have a little doubt and fear. But non-interference doesn't mean 'just do it.' Non-interference means that those things you are telling yourself, those thoughts that are going through you—they are a part of life, *it's not you*. Don't take it personally. You are being flooded with, and blessed by, life's energies that give you an ocean of emotions. It's an ocean of fascination."

"So, I should just not get caught up with my internal dialogues?"

"You don't need to get caught up in all the things that are going through your mind. In the air around you there are so many particles, if you saw them under a microscope, you would freak out at what you are breathing in and surrounded by. But the grace of life says it is not necessary for you to see that. Just breathe in oxygen and exhale carbon dioxide. You don't need to be distracted by what is floating in the space around you."

"Physically, we have been perfectly designed that way. But emotionally, the intelligence doesn't do everything for you, otherwise, there would be no fun. It gives you the freedom and choice to select emotions and ideas and feelings, and to carry them out, through daring and competence and fearlessness. To experience the invitation to life as a daring call that is pure and uncorrupted and be intrigued and fascinated by who you are. Captivated not only by what you are doing, but by who you are. If you can be absorbed in your own presence, that becomes mindfulness."

"You have been built with the capacity to enjoy life with freedom and choice. So, you have crazy, weird thoughts, that's natural. If everybody wakes up in the morning and they all come out of their houses onto the road saying, 'Good morning, I love you!' it would be a mad, mad world."

"You are never asked to do that—but you can *choose* to do it, if you want. You can choose to say what you want to yourself, or to anyone. You can choose to look in the mirror just to get the booger out of your nose and brush the snarls out of your hair. Or you can choose to see the mirror as a passageway, an invitation to unconditional love. An invitation to silent, sweet surrender."

"Silent sweet surrender means, 'I have no fight.' You are saying to your presence, 'I love you; I have no fight with you.' That will become an acknowledgment, actually, from the other side of the mirror. It's a sense you can feel. When you see yourself, you have a sense, you feel something. That feeling is very, very important. It exposes your true innocence, the true power of being who you are. You are a powerful adventurer in life."

He leaned back and looked at Mark. Mark leaned forward and put his hands on the table. His heart was pounding.

"*Who. Are. You.*"

"You will get all the answers, believe me. But first, I need a cup of coffee."

He got up, walked over to the sideboard and poured himself a cup. Mark was drumming his fingers on the arm of his chair. The door to the atrium opened behind him and there was a loud crash. A waiter had dropped a tray of dishes as he came through the doorway. Mark turned to see, and when he turned back, he saw the man entering one of the offices at the other end of the lounge.

"Oh no you don't!" he shouted as he leapt from his chair. He bolted across the lounge, banged into the office door as it was swinging shut, and burst into the room.

"Where is he?"

It was a small office. A young woman sat at a desk facing the door. On the wall behind her was a large mirror. Mark saw his own reflection, and the rest of the room, but there was no sign of the man. Mark's head jerked back and forth, eyes darting around the room.

"Who are you looking for, sir?"

"Where is he?"

The woman's hand was under her desk, hovering over a panic button.

"There's no one here, sir."

Mark looked around the room once more, stared at his reflection for a moment, then turned and hurried over to the concierge desk.

"The man I was sitting with, who is he? He's a high roller, you must know him!"

"I'm sorry, sir, I didn't see who you were with."

Mark looked around.

"Cameras! You've got security footage. You could identify him!"

"Sir, that's not available to the public. Is there a problem, sir?"

A security man had appeared next to the counter and was staring at Mark. Mark was breathing hard, glancing around the room.

"No. Sorry."

He walked across the room and out into the atrium. He was shaking, wild with anger and confusion. He walked across the lobby, scanning the crowd, breathing heavily. The security man followed several paces behind him. As Mark stepped onto the carpeted floor of the casino, the noise of the lobby began to recede, and the lighting grew dimmer. Echoing voices gave way to murmurs around the gaming tables. Music pulsed beneath the laughter and the sounds of the tables. As Mark looked around, he began to laugh, and his laughter grew and redoubled. He turned around to see the security man speaking into his wrist and laughed again. He laughed as he walked through the casino to the elevator and went up to his room to pack.

CHAPTER 12

BREAKING THE LAW

"You were born to discover."

Eric stared out the window of his hotel's rooftop lounge. The lights of the Las Vegas Strip were burning brightly. The sky was crisscrossed by the lights of airplanes arriving and leaving from McCarran Airport. A web of lighted streets spread out across the valley floor, out to the foothills to the West and East. Eric knew that beyond the pool of light that was Las Vegas, there were hundreds of miles of darkness in every direction.

He turned to the man seated across from him.

"They gave me a standing ovation."

He said it with a sense of wonder, almost disbelief.

"I knew it," said the man.

"I could feel from the start that the audience was with me, and I started to relax, and it felt very natural. Once I realized it was going over well, it became an incredible pleasure. It felt *so good* to talk to them, not as a doctor but as a human being, to talk about *life*. And at the end, they stood up. I couldn't believe it. They were cheering! I had so many people coming up to me afterwards, and they were so excited!"

"That's fantastic," said the man, "and that's just the beginning."

"That's right! Someone was talking to me about publishing it as an article."

"That's great."

"Yes, think how many people will see it! But what I'd really like to do is to develop it into a book, if I could get some backing."

“That’s a great idea. I’m sure you can find someone to help with that.”

Eric looked at the window and saw his reflection over the lights twinkling in the blackness outside.

“I feel great. I feel free. I feel like I’m starting a new life. You know, we’re here in this little, brief space called life, and beyond that is a vast, mysterious realm that we know nothing about. And maybe we can, somehow, in this life, connect with that vast unknown and make this life not so little and brief.”

“Life is not forever,” said the man, “but it is infinite. There are no limits to what you can experience and know. And if you can live that way, then death becomes not a big deal.”

“It seems strange to be talking about death now, but that’s really been the crux of my anxiety. I’m not looking forward to my death, obviously, but what really terrifies me is the fear that I’ll die without having realized what’s inside me. There’s some kind of uncharted territory, that only I can sense and explore. It probably has something to do with medicine and the heart, but I don’t really know. That’s what makes it so fascinating. I just know that I don’t want to die in the same world I lived in. I want to explore, and find something, and bring it back for the rest of the people.”

“And you will.”

“We’re not here forever, and there’s such an incredible world to experience, and yet we behave as if we’re bored and disgusted by living. Why do we do that?”

“You will never be able to appreciate your death process. You won’t appreciate dying. You don’t want to die. You are holding on. For you, the meaning of ‘life’ and ‘death’ are very different. There is a part of you that is dying every day, on a cellular level, and other levels as well. In many ways, you are playing a game of hide and seek with death. You are *denying* death. You are trying to act as if you will live forever, or at least a few more years. Your life is planned ahead for a couple of years. But death is actually playing a very weird game with you, just dancing around, dancing around. If you can really get into it, the dance with death becomes an invitation to *live.*”

"An invitation to live," said Eric, "means an appreciation for the impermanence of life."

"The life you are now engaged in is set up for only one purpose: to continue. Continuity is your goal in life. Continue from where? In your mind, it is from where you are right now—which is based on the past."

"You could say there are two worlds you live in, an inner world and an outer world. The inner world is made up of your immediate, day-to-day living, based on continuity. This inner world, like a heartbeat expanding and contracting, gives you moments of happiness and unhappiness—but never allows you to truly stretch yourself, to open outward. Billions upon billions of human beings live and die in the inner world. And then, there is an outer world which, through your fire, by breaking the boundaries, you can enter."

"You describe an inner world and an outer world, as distinct experiences of living—are they distinct states of consciousness? What are you really describing when you talk about moving from an inner world to an outer world?"

"Everything around you is in resonance, pulsating. Everywhere around you a delightful music is being played. But it's as if you are living in a closed house, while a great orchestra is playing outside, so you don't hear it clearly. This leads you to a point where you crack open a window, allowing the music from outside to faintly come inside. And then a sense comes, and you no longer hear it as coming from outside, you feel it inside you. And you begin to dance, you begin to feel good, you get into the rhythm."

"You're speaking metaphorically. When you talk about the music you feel coming from outside, and dancing with it, do you mean being in tune, in sync, with the people and things around you?"

"With the whole flow of life, and in this movement there is no time. That's why it feels magical and mystical. In your ordinary reality, you always function with a past, present and future. Movement without time becomes *space*. When you can crack time, it doesn't stay in you as a memory, so there is nothing in your system to congest you. Everything that is in your system, everything you can recall as a memory, comes from somewhere or other in time, and it brings a congestion. Your memories are making you feel congested and very heavy."

"Is there a way to shed that heaviness?"

"There are moments you have been with me in no-time. Those moments *punctured* you. That puncture, that perforation, created openings in you that allow a fresh breeze to go through you. This may sound very esoteric, but there is really no magic about breaking through time. In fact, it is the most natural thing that is possible. Understand time as a creation of the mind."

"All right," said Eric, "I'm familiar with the idea that time is a creation of the mind."

"It is possible, by breaking the boundaries of time, that you can open. The whole of life is about breaking the law. You break the boundaries, the limitations. Law is a creation, like time, of the human mind. Law is created because you are wild. To keep you in place, for the preservation of the species, you created the law. Inside of that is a rebellious kid. But you can break the boundaries of your limitations."

"It is time for you to really know about the life force and awakening. Everything that you are doing, in one way or another, is directly related to the amount of aliveness and wakefulness that you have. All the things you see or do are related in that way."

"Then aliveness and wakefulness seem to be a prerequisite, because they're what give you the energy to see other possibilities in life, right?"

"What is obvious to you is what is happening in your life right now, the things that you are worried about, the things that are making your life good or bad—all those things affect you. They have a certain kind of impact on you. But there is something else, something other than what is obvious to you, that is also influencing and affecting your life."

"What you are right now seems to be the result of what is obvious, what is available, what is in your capacity to touch. But deeper inside, deep within you like an undercurrent going through you, there is a *force*. In fact, if the force is very *clear* and strong enough—stronger than what is happening to you externally—the force itself can change the circumstances affecting your life and give you the brilliance to really *see* life."

"All right," said Eric, "to have the aliveness and wakefulness to see the true nature of life – how does that work, how do I bring that out?"

"You interact with life through your five senses. But there is more to the interaction with life than just the five senses. There are greater forces around you that you are not experiencing clearly, because there is a fog, a thin layer hovering around you like fumes, that makes you feel congested, makes you feel tight inside. That feeling is not related to what is happening in your external life."

"I think I know what you mean about the fog and the feeling of congestion. It's like there's a cloud of doubt and anxiety around me, always just under the surface. And you say that those feelings are not related to the external events in my life? How can that be?"

"When you were born, at the moment of birth itself, you were exposed to and experienced a very different energy, which is not in your memory or remembrance. What you have within you, beyond the layers of frustration and sadness, is a layer of *diffused anger*. It is like a smoke that is going around your body. It's not the same anger you experience as in a temper tantrum or going out of control. This diffused anger you won't be able to look at and say, 'I'm angry about x, y or z.'"

"We're born angry?"

"I use 'anger' as a word describing a force, not as a category of something that is bad or undesirable. Anger is a force which comes into play from the very beginning of life. It has no psychological, mental or emotional basis. You are not angry *about* something."

"It is fascinating to see how it plays a part in the marvelous orchestra of the elements and forces of life, how it is all set up. Of all the forces you have access to, one of the greatest is your anger. You are damned angry, and you don't realize it. You know you are angry only when someone gets you to explode—but that's not the same anger I am talking about here. *Right now* you are damned angry, and you don't know it. And that anger—like your sadness and sorrow—doesn't belong to you. It's not actually an anger that is coming out of you, personally, it is a *force*. It is a force you have had since the day you were born."

"Is it anger at having to leave the womb?"

"Inside the womb, during the months you'll never remember, you had the greatest interaction with sound and motion. Before you were born means what? Before you opened your eyes for the light to go through you. Before you were born, sound and light took care of you. Inside the womb, what do you see? You are in touch. You *feel* the sound. Seen from the outside, the womb appears dark, due to the contrast with the light we are familiar with. But inside the womb, for the life that is forming, the womb is not dark. There is no contrast, there is no darkness. The darkness exists because you compare, because of your duality. For the forming life, the touch of light is there, there is no darkness. Then what happens? When your time is ready, you come out."

"What is the real impact of leaving the known territory? The true meaning of surrender is, leaving the known territory. Birth means what? Surrender to life. Leaving the womb means leaving the known territory. And suddenly, the baby is crying. There are many reasons for that, but the *real* reason is something you never ever thought. The first thing that happens for the new life coming into the world is, when it opens its eyes, the *fire* goes into them. The fire comes in the breath and in the light. You are greeted with light, the light welcomes you. The welcoming energy, the light the newborn baby sees with its eyes newly opened, is a light still coming through fire. It is not a pure light, it is not an infinite light, it is not the same as the light that the baby knew in the womb."

"What do you mean by pure light?"

"There are two distinct types of light I am talking about. The first is the light we are all familiar with: physical light, light that comes from combustion – the sun, light bulbs, fire—all these come from burning, and they give heat as well as light. The other light is what I call pure light, cool light, infinite light. This is the light of creation, the ultimate nature of all things. It does not consume, and it has no source. When the baby is born, it is the warm light that greets the baby. Inside the womb, it is the pure light, the infinite light, that holds the baby."

"We were in touch with something in the womb. What was it?"

"You were closest to the five elements—earth, fire, water, air and space, when you were inside the womb. You surrender to birth and immediately what happens is, you are *cut off.* Cut off from what? Boom-boom, boom-boom, boom-boom—the sound. The immediate thing you lose is the heartbeat that was with you for all those months, the motion, the rhythm of life. And what you are trying to do now with life is, you are attempting to create a closeness with the elements that you once knew before. You can't go back and do it, but you can recreate it now, in order to get in touch. Deep inside, you know that if you bring the elements so close to you— the earth, fire, water, air and space—everything that was compressed together and touching you inside the womb—if you do that, the pure light will come to you. And you will know everything. You knew everything before you were born."

Eric asked, "When you say, 'You will know everything,' do you mean having a connection to infinite intelligence? Does that come with being in touch with the elements?"

"One of the most magnificent things about the forces and the elements is that when you realize how the elements within you come into play with the motion, sound and light, then life will make total sense to you. Remember, I talked about the elements and the forces interacting? Motion, sound and light are the three forces that you relate to in this life."

"From the moment you leave the womb, what you feel is anger. Anger at being *out of place*. You feel out of place. It's not psychological or emotional. When you feel out of place, an imbalance comes. If you are in place, you will never be angry. You can't be. Any time you see anger coming it means what? You are out of place. You feel you don't belong there. Because of the sense that you don't belong there, you attempt to fit in. You attempt to belong because you feel you are out of place and you don't want to feel that way."

"What you are trying to do is, you are trying to be loved. Not to love—you are trying to *be* loved. Your real true desire is to be loved—'Please love me!' That is because you feel out of place. And that's the beauty of it. It is only through awareness of the elements and forces that you can break it."

"Let me review this," said Eric, "We have a residual feeling of being separated, apart, out of place, because of our separation from the womb. And so in life, we have a yearning to be loved, in order to feel a sense of unity and connection. But we have this built-in, or born-in, feeling of being out of place, apart. Can we ever overcome that feeling?"

"Out of the need to be loved out of place comes *identity*. The baby doesn't have an identity. Identity comes because of separation, being out of place. The baby inside the womb was one with the elements and the forces, dancing together. There was no separation whatsoever. The baby you once were was one with everything through your mother's womb. You were one with the whole universe. In that oneness, you didn't have an identity. The reference point, the identity, comes when you are displaced. When you are in place, there is no reference point and no identity."

"The environment of the womb is so different from this world we live in after we're born," said Eric, "that it must be an incredibly traumatic event to be taken out of the womb and put into this external reality that's so dangerous and complicated and separated. So, we have an anger, and a sadness, that we experienced before we were fully conscious, from the experience of our birth. Are those emotions of anger and yearning an inherent, inevitable part of our human existence, or can we somehow be free of them, or transform them?"

"What is your anger, really? It is trapped sound. The sound is trapped. You are choking, actually. There is another sound that wants to come, but it is cut off, it falls. The force of life was trying to rise, and it was cut off—it was blocked—and it falls back to earth. It's important to understand that, if you can. You have a fracture inside you, something broke inside you, and your life force got cut."

"When the anger comes, for you it is not in a pure state, it is not clean. If you can have a very clean anger— if you can get angry for no reason—that's great, because it becomes just a *force* then. It has no object, no target to hit. The moment your anger is directed at somebody or something, it no longer goes up, it gets attached and recycles its force downward. But if you get really, really, angry, you are *aroused*. You are very aroused, very alive, you would jump out of your skin if you could."

"That's the force. The force is always the same, it's the way it's directed that matters. If you have anger without a reference point, then it doesn't become anger. In fact, the sexual arousal you feel, when you get very aroused, that is truly anger without a reference—it's an ignition. The life force ignites within you, and the fire brings heat and illumination, and brilliance comes out of it."

"This is very personal," said Eric, "but sometimes my wife and I will be arguing, fighting about one thing or another, and very quickly we go from arguing to making love."

The man smiled and nodded.

"At a certain time in your development as you are growing up, the first thing you learn is how to manipulate—you learn how to cheat. The first thing you learn in the mastery of life is how to find your way, how to get what you want. We call it being a spoiled brat, crying to get attention, being bad, whatever it is, but what gives you the energy, or provides the fuel, to do that? It is the anger, the diffused anger. It is invisible, untouchable, without a source. If you touch the deepest silence someday, if you become very alive, the one thing you will see is that your anger has evaporated."

"You have the anger, and you have the sadness. The gap between the anger and the sadness is called *shame*. Unbearable shame. Shame is a very fascinating thing. It is actually because there is the creation of shame and anger that you have the possibility of destroying them. That is the adventure and the beauty of being a spiritual warrior. It's not just trying to play a game of hide-and-seek with your life and with death."

"When the tears of sadness evaporate, they become compassion and warmth. When the flames of anger disappear, they manifest as wisdom, and your brilliance will come out."

"So, the anger and sadness are keeping me from seeing?"

"You don't have clarity in your life right now because the lid of diffused anger is blocking you. It's not that you are not bright enough, or you are not energetic enough, or good enough, or anything like that. The diffused anger stops you."

"Many times, you have mistaken the diffused anger for sadness, and then, in a very interesting way, the sadness comes into play. You are not just sad because you are separated or cut off. You have not just a sorrow or a grief, you also have a very different form of sadness—a sadness that you are angry. You are in deep sadness that you are angry, because within you the force is trying to lift you up. It is saying to you, showing you that it wants you to rise up. It really wants you to rise. And you recognize somewhere the diffused anger, and there is a recognition that you are sad that you are so angry inside. That makes you mad. It is a very quick, geometric progression."

"It seems hard to escape that process. What's beneath all the sadness and anger?"

"Deep inside, you have a sense of a basic goodness coming from the very bottom layer of the foundation, the fire from the earth itself, from the body itself. There is a deep sense that is there. You are born to *live*. You are not just born to die; you are not an animal. You are born to be divine. And the force itself is so powerful it makes you know that. It is not a knowledge, it's not information. It makes you *feel* that."

"It's hard for me to feel that, and that's very frustrating."

"You wish that you were not an angry person. Deep within you, beyond all the games you are playing and all the toughness you display, there is a little baby who knows that there is nothing else you want to do but fall in love and embrace life. You develop an unbelievable amount of armor, mentally and emotionally, in every way, to somehow keep this form that you've created, the anger. You rationalize and justify all the things you have done. Otherwise you will look like a fool—not to anyone else—to yourself. You are afraid to see a fool in the mirror, so you somehow or other justify yourself. When you see yourself in the mirror, you may see a spiritual person or an innocent person or whatever. But in truth there is nobody in the mirror. You are looking at nobody."

"At your birth, by the force of nature, you surrendered one territory. You were born. If you'd had a choice, you would still be in the womb! In the passage you have taken from the time of your birth up until now, there are three things you are trying to get in touch with. The first thing you are trying to get in touch with is the *heartbeat*. Then there is the sound, which is what gives you balance and a sense of connection to your matrix. Then there is the light, the true nature of life."

"In your life, how that translates is by the intimacy you experience. The manifestation of the heartbeat in your life is the intimacy that you have with a man or a woman and the family. It's not that you are going back to the womb—you are *recreating* the womb. You are recreating the motion and the sound."

"As a forming life, you had no sense of contrast or duality about anything. You didn't think it was dark in the womb and that you came out into the light. There was no duality. A desperate attempt is being made to create a womb in this world so there will be no darkness. And that is a very deep drive within you. You are trying to recreate the womb, and you are having a hell of a lot of trouble with it. That has been your passage since birth."

"The force of life itself, by its very nature, not only makes you very alive, very aroused and alert, but it also opens your porous nature. A moment of intimacy is a moment when you are porous. It's like a static charge, where your hair rises. Your porous units become available to open, allowing the breeze to go through you."

"You came to the womb invisible. You became visible at the point of conception because you were porous. And the deepest meaning of intimacy is, you are creating the world, creating the womb, in which your porous units can become open to let the breeze go through you. Awakening is not a state. It is a deep passage of the fire to a brilliance of opening. That's the invitation life has brought you, and that is worth living for."

"Yes," whispered Eric.

"It is never by going back to the womb that you will wake up and become alive. Getting in touch with the forces right now—with the motion and the sound and light—will allow you to see the light. And you will know indeed that you never left the womb, that the womb is still there with you. That's why you were born. You were born to *discover*. Born to see that you create everything, that all creation is with you together. You are never left alone in any part of creation. You are always included. You are always there."

Eric stared into the deep blackness outside the window. He felt a sense of awe, and deep gratitude.

"I always felt that life was a realm of infinite possibility, but not for me. I always felt there were great things to be discovered—but not by me, even though that is what I most want. I always doubted, always felt like something was lacking in me. But that's not unique to me, is it? We all have unworthiness, doubt, fear. Some people just go forward in spite of all that, because their passion and fascination is so strong that they don't care anymore. I want that to be me."

"That is you. You are a great man."

"And it's a great life," said Eric, "whoever you are, you brought me back to life. I can't possibly thank you for what you've given me. I'll never forget this time, and I hope I never lose what I've found."

"This is just the beginning," said the man, "so we better get moving."

He beckoned to the waiter, gave him some bills, and the two men walked out of the lounge.

As they walked to the elevator lobby, the man gestured toward the men's room.

"I have to go."

Eric waited by the bar entrance as the man went into the bathroom. He felt there was more he needed to say to properly express his gratitude and awe. He rehearsed in his mind what he wanted to say. He waited like this for several minutes and the man still did not return. He started to wonder if something was wrong—maybe he was ill. He walked over to the men's room and pushed the door open. As he entered, he saw that the water was running in all four of the sinks. The room appeared to be empty.

"Hello? Is everything all right?"

There was no answer. He walked over to the stalls and looked in each one. They were empty. He walked back to the sinks. One by one the water shut off in each. When Eric had visited the bathroom earlier, there had been several men using the facilities. There was no one here now, and no sounds. Eric stood in front of a sink and looked at his reflection in the mirror. He put his left hand over his heart and with his right hand he touched the mirror. He stood like this for a long time, then he smiled at his reflection, put his hands together in a gesture of prayer, and bowed his head.

"Thank you," he said, and turned to leave.

At that moment another man entered, and the sounds of the bar flooded in through the open door. Eric walked back to the bar entrance. He looked around in the bar, though he knew he would not see the man, not now and never again. He smiled, shook his head and laughed as he made his way to the elevator.

Epilogue

The morning was bright and clear. Mark's flight was leaving in two hours. He knew the ride to the airport was a short one, and he would have some time to kill before his flight, but he had said his goodbyes to the hotel and was anxious to begin his journey home.

He had eaten breakfast at the buffet, at the same table he had shared with the stranger several days earlier. After breakfast, he walked through the hotel and the casino, silently revisiting the places where he had sat and listened to the man. He visited the garden café, the piano bar, the pool, the lakeside café, and the VIP lounge, and at each place he summoned back all that he could remember of the stranger's words and his own emotions and insights.

Mark felt changed, but not as if he had gained something. Rather, he felt a curious absence, as if familiar patterns of thinking and feeling were no longer operating within him. He did not notice this at first, but at a certain moment as he was walking through the casino, he stopped and said to himself, "I'm full of silence."

He thought of his wife, and there was a calmness in his thoughts. He felt no guilt or anger, only love.

On Monday, he would return to work. He looked forward to this with relish, as if he were trading one casino for another, equally exciting one.

After he completed his circuit of the hotel, he returned to his room and fetched his bags. The ride to the airport was indeed brief, and the check-in and security line were also quickly passed.

When he reached the gate for his flight, he looked around and saw that Eric was not there yet. He was not surprised; it was still early. He went to a coffee bar where he could see the waiting area for his gate. He was anxious to see Eric and share with him what he had experienced that week. He rehearsed in his mind how he might explain the extraordinary events and insights he had absorbed. He realized that he admired Eric very much, and he wanted his respect. He didn't want him to think he was a crackpot. He opened his bag, got out a pad and pen, and wrote a series of bullet point notes.

- Patience, focus, fascination replace greed, restlessness, fear
- Sensing vs. guessing
- Hollow bamboo
- Everything exists as a flow
- Fascination
- Non-interference, freedom and choice, unconditional love
- Blue carpet
- Impossible is possible
- Imperfection, impermanence, unpredictability
- Born to play
- Spontaneity
- Innocence
- Motion, sound and light
- We are an ocean of emotion
- Nothing is too good to be true

Eventually, the call came to begin boarding. Eric had still not appeared. Mark walked to the gate and was soon taking his seat on the plane. He turned in his seat and looked down the aisle at the passengers filing in. The mood was distinctly different from the inbound flight. This crowd was more sedate. Some looked tired and happy, some looked hung over.

After several minutes, nearly everyone was seated. An attendant was about to close the door when Eric appeared, red-faced and out of breath. He made his way up the aisle, muttering, "Excuse me, sorry, excuse me." He found his row and smiled when he saw Mark.

"I made it!"

"You made it! Hey, man, I didn't think you were coming."

"I got the time wrong! I thought the flight was an hour later. When I got here, I barely had time to check in and get up here."

"I'm glad you made it. How was your conference?"

"Well,"

At that moment the captain announced that they were preparing for takeoff, and the roar of the engines rose steadily in volume. The plane taxied, turned, and raced down the runway and up into the air. They were pushed back into their seats by the acceleration, and Eric gripped his armrest and gritted his teeth.

Soon the plane leveled off, the noise diminished, and the seat belt sign chimed off.

"Whew!" said Eric, "I always have trouble with that. Okay. So, you were asking about the conference. Well, I have to tell you, the conference, and the whole trip, has been one of the most extraordinary experiences of my life. I want to tell you about it, but I hardly know where to begin."

"Really! Well, I want to hear all about it, and I've got an incredible story to tell *you.*"

"Oh? Did you win a lot?"

Mark laughed.

"You could say that. Listen, we've got a long flight ahead of us, and before I get into it, I need a drink."

"It's a little early, isn't it?"

"I don't care. And you're having one, too."

He hailed the flight attendant and ordered two beers. He looked out the window. The plane had just emerged from the cloud cover, and the sun reflected blindingly on the tops of the clouds, rolling fields of white stretching out to the horizon. Their drinks arrived. Mark drained his glass and let out a sigh of satisfaction.

"Now then," he said, and began his story.

www.ingramcontent.com/pod-product-compliance
Lightning Source LLC
Chambersburg PA
CBHW030414310726
48979CB00002B/407